A SANGUINE GEM

A SANGUINE GEM

A MARSDEN ROMANCE BOOK THREE

DAWN BROWER

MONARCHAL GLENN PRESS

This is a work of fiction. Names, characters, places, and incidents are products of the author's imagination or are used fictitiously and are not to be construed as real. Any resemblance to actual locales, organizations, or persons, living or dead, is entirely coincidental.

CONTENTS

In life we are faced with many choices. One of the best choices I made was starting to write. Above that the only thing that tops it is my two boys. Luke and Nathan I love you so much and you are truly the biggest blessing and best thing to come into my life.

CHAPTER ONE

*L*iam Marsden had a lot of things on his mind. However, he couldn't dwell on what was beyond his control. He had more pressing issues to deal with, starting with a meeting his father demanded. He had never let him down before, and he had no intention of starting at this juncture of his life.

He walked into his family home and strolled down the hallway towards the study. As he opened the door, he got a brief look at his father engrossed in his own work. The viscount had his dark hair pulled back at the nape of his neck; loose strands fell over his forehead as he tilted his head to read the paper in front of him. Liam had always admired his tenacity and willingness to do anything to accomplish any task. He didn't give up easily and believed the world belonged to him to take what he wanted from it.

"Ah good you're here," He glanced up at Liam and set his work aside. "I have a few things I need to discuss with you."

"I came as soon as I received your missive. What's so urgent?"

"A good number of things that I didn't foresee."

On closer scrutiny, Liam could see stress lines forming on his father's face. His eyes filled with worry as he rubbed his temples. What could have happened to make him appear so concerned? Liam didn't think this meeting would be a jovial one. His father didn't often worry about things. No, Viscount Torrington took action and left the fretting to others.

"This is serious?" Liam asked as he raised an eyebrow.

"I received a letter from your sister. Some of it is good news. Most of it is actually."

"It's the part that isn't good news that concerns you." Liam sat down and leaned forward, giving his father his full attention. "What has happened?"

"First, I should tell you that you are the proud uncle of a strapping baby boy. You sister had her child a month ago. They named him William Jamieson after his two grandfathers. Poor boy has a lot to live up to with that name." He laughed.

"If I'm an uncle that means you are a grandfather. How does that make you feel old man" Liam grinned. He couldn't resist an opportunity to tease his father.

"Bite your tongue, boy. It'll be a long time before I'm an old man," With a devilish grin on his face, his father sat back in his chair and studied Liam. "This is good for you because I don't think you are quite ready to fill my shoes."

Liam hoped his father lived a very long life. He couldn't imagine a life without the man's robust personality filling a room wherever he went. Like most children, he believed his parents infallible. He knew they were mere human beings, but he liked to believe they would live forever.

"No, I can't say I'm in a hurry to take the reins from you. I pray you're here for many years to come. For more reasons than one," Liam said. "But regardless of how I feel about your possible demise that isn't why you summoned me here. Nor is it the news about my new nephew. Grateful as I am to hear about it, something else weighs on your mind. I think it's time to dispense with the pleasantries."

"That isn't all your sister wrote about," he said with a heavy sigh. "She has some concerns that she asked me to look into."

"Is it about the merger of Marsden Shipping with RandCo? There isn't an issue with its completion, is there?" He needed to dispense with that bit of concern first because it was at the forefront of his mind. "If so, I'd like to take care of it immediately."

"No, that at least is going well. We should have considered a merger as soon as Lily and Rand married." Viscount Torrington sighed and stood up. He strolled over to a nearby shelf and pulled out a decanter of brandy along with two glasses. "This is something entirely different and I'm not sure how to proceed."

"What's Lily worried about?" Liam's concern rose. What could be so dreadful?

Viscount Torrington handed Liam a brandy filled snifter. He took a sip of his own and set it down. He stared past Liam, his eyes unfocused. "The Earl of Devon was a pretty good friend of mine."

"I remember." Liam nodded.

"At one time I'd hope to have a merger with him," his father paused and stared down at his drink. "It was the reason we attempted to betroth you and Gemma."

Liam would rather forget about that time in his life. He grimaced and stared up at his father. "Right, that was several years ago." What was his father getting at?

"The business merger and familial one fell through at the same time. We never found a reason to revisit either." He downed the rest of his drink in his glass. "I have to admit a part of me is glad it didn't. As much as I liked the man I abhor the gentleman who inherited his estate."

Liam rubbed his temple; a pain throbbed through his head listening to his father rattle on. "What does Alfie have to do with this?"

"Lady Gemma is my concern."

She wasn't his, so Liam had no clue why he brought her into the conversation. In fact, everything he'd said so far hadn't made any sense to him.

"Father, what exactly is the problem?" Frustration built to the boiling point deep inside him. "I don't understand what Lady Gemma has to do with all of this."

"Lady Gemma keeps in touch with Lily. She wrote your sister about some disturbing news." The viscount sat back and studied Liam. He steepled his hands together as he spoke. "She thinks I might have a solution to the problem. I can think of a couple of ways we could assist her, but you would have to be willing."

"What it is you would like me to do?" Liam replied, a horrible feeling sinking to the bottom of his gut.

Viscount Torrington leaned forward and set his hands on his desk. His eyes bore into Liam's as he appeared to weigh over the issue that troubled him.

"You know I'd never force you to do anything, but I think in this you believe as I do."

"I'm at a loss as you haven't explained anything to me," Liam reminded him. "How am I to know if I agree or not if you don't?" He silently hoped his father wasn't about to ask what he thought he was. After he mentioned the botched attempt to betroth him to Lady Gemma, Liam couldn't help but wonder —he couldn't possibly want him to marry Gemma. *Could he?*

"First, you should be aware of the circumstances regarding Lady Gemma and why Lily is so concerned," his father told him. "Then I will explain my idea and the two possible solutions to it. One is a better option, and the other should only be considered if you are against the first."

"And what is happening with her?" Liam stood up and paced around the room. He stopped a few steps away and pinned his father with a stare. "Quit stalling and tell me what's going on."

"Alfie is—being difficult."

"In what way?"

If his father didn't tell him what was going on soon. Liam wouldn't be held responsible for his actions. Their conversation was driving him mad.

"He has squandered the entire inheritance. If the estate weren't entailed, he'd sell it to pay off his enormous debts. That leaves him in a bit of a bind. He needs money and as fast as possible."

Liam nodded. "I think I see the correlation. Lady Gemma still has an inheritance, and he wants to get his hands on it."

Viscount Torrington stood up and joined him in front of the desk. His eyes had an angry edge to them. Liam knew his father well enough to realize he wanted to do some damage to the new Earl of Devon. Whatever Alfie was doing enraged him. Liam had a bad feeling about what was going on with Lily's friend.

"In a manner of speaking yes and he is willing to use whatever is at his disposal to get it. Lady Gemma is afraid he might force the situation to get his way."

"I see." Liam scowled. "Does she have reason to believe he will act so dishonorably?"

"This is old news." His father frowned and crossed his arms over his chest. "I got the letter today from your sister. It might already be a foregone conclusion. I'm afraid we may be too late with how slow mail travels between England and America. I don't know what we'll find if we go to the Earl of Devon's estate."

Not good news, in fact, they were quite horrid. Liam might have issues with Lady Gemma, but he'd never wanted anyone to hurt her. He'd willingly help her deal with her cousin if he could find a good solution to her problem.

"I hadn't even considered that. We are wasting time. What are your solutions?" Liam asked.

"Lady Gemma needs a husband. She doesn't gain majority and control over her funds for five more years. She only has one solution that will effectively work for her."

With those words, Liam's fears were realized. His heart beat faster in his chest and the pounding in his head intensified.

His father wanted him to marry Lady Gemma.

Liam should be appalled at the suggestion, especially as he'd already tried to betroth them when they were younger. He had never denied that Lady Gemma had beauty in spades. She had luxurious crimson hair and eyes the color of jade. His mouth watered thinking about her beautiful complexion and soft curves. That was until she open her mouth to speak. Listening to her droll on and on for what seemed like forever, he invariably forgot how exquisite her body and face appeared and wanted to put some much needed distance between them.

Why should he sacrifice his life for her?

The brazen redhead had been the bane of his existence for several years now. It took the death of her father for her to back away. Admittedly he admired her tenacity and willingness to make her wishes known, but that didn't mean he ever desired to tie himself to her forever. Perhaps his father's other solution would be easier for him to stomach.

"You are not suggesting what I think you are." Appalled, Liam sat back down in his chair. Shock filled him to the brink. He had to be reading the situation wrong.

"I had hoped that you had some tender feelings for the chit. You are constantly arguing with her." His father sat back down in his chair, a slight knowing smirk resting on his face. "That is a form of passion. Trust me I know a bit about denial in that area."

"Well, you're incorrect in your assumption." Liam

glared. He didn't have any feelings for Gemma. She was a nuisance nothing more. "There aren't any tender feelings on either side. The girl irritates me to no end. I never did understand what Lily saw in her."

"That's too bad. I still have the betrothal contract I signed with Lady Gemma's father. We could have used it to our advantage."

Liam stared at his father with a blank expression. He'd actually signed the contract? How could he have done that? His father had reassured him he'd never force him to marry anyone.

"Excuse me could you repeat that? I don't think I heard you correctly." Liam hoped he'd heard wrong. Sadly he doubted he had. "You informed me the betrothal hadn't been finalized."

"That's correct," His father grinned. "However Devon hoped I'd change my mind and told me to keep the contract. All I have to do to make it legal is sign my name to it."

Liam blanched. His father was losing his mind. There wasn't a chance in hell he'd make him marry Lady Gemma. "But you're not going to, right

"So you are not willing to help?"

"I didn't say that." Liam shook his head. "I'm willing to hear the other plan you have. I'm hoping it is preferable to the latter."

"The other plan involves you basically kidnapping the girl and taking her to your sister in South Carolina."

Relief flooded him at his father's words. Calm now that the storm of anxiety fled his stomach, Liam took a deep breath and considered his father's other idea. He had to agree that the second plan held more appeal. It was preferable, but not that much better in the grand scheme of things. He would still be forced to spend a considerable amount of time in Lady Gemma's company. How would he be able to get through a voyage with her? They would have to take the Sea Rover for the crossing. No other ships were available, and their steamships were only in the planning stages of being built. If he had any luck, it wouldn't take more than three weeks to complete.

The bonus, of course, would be to see his sister and his new nephew. He sincerely wished to see them so that no price was too high for him to be able to spend time in their company. He would even be willing to get to know his brother-in-law as well. Maybe he would find a way to like the rat bastard. His father may have forgiven him for stealing Lily, but Liam didn't feel like he deserved such absolution. The man had a lot of audacity to run away with the daughter of Viscount Torrington—a former pirate. Liam would give him that much.

"That plan is more conceivable to accomplish," Liam said. "But is kidnapping really necessary? Do you believe Lady Gemma will be unwilling to go to live with Lily?"

"I honestly do not know," his father sighed. "I hate to tell you this, but I think you're going to need ammunition to get her out."

"Explain," Liam demanded.

"If you go in prepared Alfie won't have anything to argue about."

"How do you suggest I do that?"

His father grinned. It almost had a wicked tinge to it. "I'm going to sign this betrothal. Go to the bishop and demand a special license. With the right amount of money and the betrothal as evidence, he won't deny you."

"I fail to see why I need to go to such lengths."

"Alfie won't let Gemma go willingly. You're going to have to force his hand." His father paused and looked him in the eye. "I'm not telling you to marry the girl. Just use the tools I'm giving you to save her."

"All right I will go see the bishop now. Afterward, I will retrieve Gemma and bring her back here to plan our next move." Liam said.

"Good. I'd hate to disappoint your sister. I hope we are not too late to help Lady Gemma."

With those words, Liam got up and walked out of the study. He had never been a fan of Lady Gemma Kemsley, but he had never wished her ill will either. If she had more trouble than she could handle, Liam had no choice but to help her. His sister depended on him, and he had never let her down before—he certainly didn't plan on starting with Lady Gemma.

The chit had better be prepared to do everything necessary to leave her home. Liam didn't suffer fools and luckily for him he knew that she didn't either. No matter what he believed, her to be he had always been able to see the keen intelligence in her eyes. Perhaps with age she had also gained some maturity to go along with it.

CHAPTER TWO

Gemma Kemsley couldn't believe her rotten luck as she strolled into the sitting room on her father's—her cousin's estate. She still had trouble wrapping her mind around the fact that her father passed away eighteen months ago. Her cousin, Alfie, inherited the title and the entailed estates upon his death. He also became her guardian. A reality that Gemma loathed for many reasons, the biggest being he had lecherous intentions towards her.

He said in no uncertain terms she would be his wife whether she liked it or not. Well, Gemma didn't like it and vowed to find a way to escape his plans for her. She took a page out of her best friend Lily's book and started to scheme her way out of the situation. The only option for her would be to run away and live in America. Lily would welcome her into her home. She just needed to find a way to leave without Alfie knowing what she had in mind.

"Ah, there you are Gemma, dear. We have some things to discuss."

Disgust filled her at the sight of her cousin invading her space. He smelled just as foul, like a night of overindulging in cheap liquor. Bloody hell, why couldn't he be in London at one of his clubs? They probably wouldn't admit him anymore. No doubt the whole ton had begun to realize the new Earl of Devon was headed to debtors' prison. It couldn't happen soon enough to satisfy her. The horrid man continued to harass her on a daily basis. She didn't know how much longer she could stand to put up with his unwanted advances.

Why did her father have to die and leave her in Alfie's care? She missed him every day. Living without him was hard enough, but to constantly have to defend herself rattled her to her very core.

"As far as I'm concerned we have talked more than I have ever liked. Go away Alfie I am not in the mood to fend off your licentious advances today," Gemma told him.

"I don't care what you want, dear. I came to

inform you that your time is up. At the end of the week, we will wed. Just as soon as I can obtain a special license." His eyes leered over her bosom as he delivered the awful news. "You look especially lovely today. How about we seal the deal with a kiss?"

Lovely? Like that was going to work on her. She'd rather stand outside in a lightning storm and beg to be struck dead than marry her cousin. Kiss him? Not bloody going to happen.

Alfie reached for her. Gemma took a step back to prevent being held in his embrace. She knew it wouldn't stop at a kiss. No, her cousin wanted to do more than press his lips on hers. He wanted to ravish her until she no longer retained any shred of innocence.

Alfie believed she owed him because he allowed her to live with him after he moved in. As her guardian, he got a stipend to provide for her living expenses. He couldn't touch the majority of her inheritance without a valid reason.

Thankfully her mother had left her a large sum of money upon her death. Only marriage or reaching her majority would allow her access to it though.

It took her a while, but she finally understood why her best friend, Lily, had been so against marriage. It was unbelievably ironic that she succumbed to it as soon as she left England, but that didn't make her argument against matrimony any less valid.

"I'd rather kiss a dead fish than allow you anywhere near me." She gave him a scathing look and frowned at him.

Heat filled her cheeks at the idea of him touching her. Not in a good way either. She didn't desire him; rather she wanted never to lay eyes on him ever again. Alfie was the exact opposite of the man she truly wanted—or rather used to long for.

"No reason to be so vicious. You'll like it once I warm you up a bit," he said, an evil grin on his lips.

In her haste to get away from him she tripped and fell backward on the settee. She tried to get up before he could take advantage of the situation, but her efforts were futile. He pounced on her after her misfortunate collapse. His lips pressed hard against hers. When she tried to open her mouth to scream he pushed his tongue inside her mouth and squeezed her breast in the palm of his hand.

Pain shot through her and continued to spread through her nipple. Alfie pulled her onto him and grinded himself against her stomach. She could feel his hardness as he rubbed himself on her. She'd lose the contents of her stomach soon if she couldn't get him to let her go.

What could she do? Not a lot of options were making themselves known to her and she was fast running out of time. An idea came to her as Alfie pushed his tongue into her mouth again. Gemma bit down on his lip and drew blood. She could taste it as a small drop fell on her tongue, it was bitter and disgusting.

"You little bitch," he shouted with rage. "You're going to pay for that."

He yanked Gemma's dress and tore the side of her bodice. He reached forward and pinched her nipple between his forefinger and thumb. She screamed out as his nails dug into the sensitive tip. She had to put some distance between them before something she couldn't escape from happened. It was clear Alfie planned on claiming her against her will.

Gemma grabbed his arm, her nails digging in and leaving half-moon imprints into his flesh. She yanked his arm away from her, ripping his hand off her bruised breast. She fought to get away from him, but it was a struggle she was losing. Her cousin was too strong, and she didn't have the ability to fight him. Tears started to fall from the corner of her eyes.

This was wrong, so very wrong, and Gemma couldn't stop it from happening to her.

"Alfie, Ole' Chap, I do hope you are not doing what I think you are."

That voice—Gemma knew that voice. Her heart raced in her chest and tingles of fire danced across her stomach. It haunted her dreams and made her want things she knew she'd never have. Alfie let her go, and she fell back on the settee. She jerked her bodice over her exposed breast, embarrassment settling in the bottom of her stomach like a dead weight.

Gemma looked over and straight into the stormy blue eyes of the only man she had ever wanted—ever allowed herself to love. His pale blond hair hung loosely over his collar making her want to run her fingers through it. She knew that the fine blond strands would be silky if she'd were to touch them.

At one time, she believed he would be her every-thing, the one person she was meant to spend the rest of her life with.

Too bad he didn't return her feelings.

No man had ever compared to him—no one ever would. This man standing in front of her, glaring at her cousin, filled her with desire and longing. Liam Marsden had ruined her for anyone else.

"I don't know why you feel comfortable waltzing in, but Gemma and I were in the middle of something. You can show yourself out the same way you came in," Alfie said.

Fool. Liam Marsden didn't take orders.

Gemma didn't know why her cousin even thought that nonsense had a possibility of working. She was simultaneously irritated and relieved Liam had showed up. She didn't know why he came out to the country, but he had saved her from ruin. She might be perpetually angry with him—but now, she'd have to set that annoyance aside to thank him. Gemma owed him a debt she didn't think she'd ever be able to repay.

"Well, I came to see my fiancée. I have to say I don't like that I walked into you getting rough with her. Explain yourself, man, before I commit murder."

Fiancée? She stood up her gaze whipping toward Liam's. A blaze of longing rushed through her with that one word. What the bloody hell was Liam talking about? The only place he had ever asked her to marry him had been in her dreams.

Sadly, in reality he ignored her whenever she came near him.

So this little announcement of his baffled her. What was the man up to? Did he know something about her situation and decided to come and save her? It wouldn't work as much as she wanted it to. Claiming to be her fiancé wouldn't make Alfie let go of her. He'd fight Liam every step of the way unless there was proof of his prior claim.

"Gemma is not your fiancée," Alfie said. He sneered, evil apparent in his gaze. "I think I'd know if I had approved of someone for her to marry."

"That's because you didn't approve it." Liam folded his arms across his chest. He oozed smugness as he looked Alfie in the eye.

Gemma hid a smile. That had to goad her cousin a bit.

"Then you can leave. I'm the only one who can approve who Gemma marries." Alfie waved his hand attempting to dismiss Liam.

Liam ignored him and stalked forward. "Her father signed the contract before he died." He turned and gave her a glance that scorched her from the inside out. Gemma only barely restrained from fanning herself. "I have waited patiently for her mourning to end so we can be married. I think it's time that we proceeded with our plans."

"What contract? Why wasn't I made aware of this?" Alfie asked as he glared at Gemma.

Gemma just shrugged her shoulders in his

general direction. She didn't have the answers he sought. She didn't have any idea what Liam was talking about. Surely her father would have told her if he had signed a contract for her to marry someone. This had to be some ruse on Liam's part. Whatever he planned she had every intention of following along with it. Anything to help her get away from her cousin would be very much preferable to submitting to his licentious groping.

"I have it right here," Liam said as he shoved the contract at Alfie. "The old earl's signature is at the bottom giving permission for me to marry his daughter, Lady Gemma Kemsley."

"I don't understand. Why didn't the solicitors tell me about this?" Alfie asked, his face turning three different shades of red.

Liam had the contract in his hands and Alfie attempted to snatch it from him. Liam just shook his head and folded it back up, placing it back in the safety of his inside pocket. Cool, calm, and collected —that was Liam.

"Possibly because they didn't know. This document has been in my father's keeping since I was fourteen years old. They decided to betroth us several years ago." Confidence intertwined with each word he spoke. "Good for business you know. We had no idea Gemma's father would die so tragically before he could tell her about it. It's sad, but well I think it's time we move on."

"I don't care." Alfie stomped his foot like a small child. "I don't approve and Gemma isn't going to marry you."

Gemma had to restrain herself from laughing at the ridiculous situation she found herself in. The only man she had ever loved demanded she marry him and her libertine cousin thought he had a chance of denying it. Not for a minute did she believe the contract had any validity to it. Lily had to have put Liam up to the scheme to help her escape. Gemma knew that Liam didn't want her. She'd learned it the hard way two years ago. It didn't matter though; he was here to save her. She knew Liam would do anything his twin sister asked him. They'd always been close. If she demanded he save her best friend he'd do it without blinking. Liam wouldn't be in her ancestral home stepping in between her and Alfie otherwise.

"Seems like you don't have any say in the matter, Alfie," Gemma said solemnly. "Papa signed the contract. That supersedes your wishes. I have no choice, but to marry Liam Marsden."

This was surely a dream. Marry him? A flutter of

hope started to ignite within her. She squashed it before it could take root. Liam wasn't going to marry her. Gemma refused to give in to something surely destined to destroy her. Hope was an evil four letter word, designed to bring a person to their knees and wrap them up in despair.

"You could refuse him."

"I don't want to." Gemma laughed.

Alfie clenched his fists at his side. His hand flew up and stopped in midair as if he rethought the action he'd been about to take. He glanced over at Liam and Gemma did as well. He was in a position to strike. Alfie would never have gotten the slap across Gemma's cheek.

Gemma grinned with relief. Alfie would have to find some other heiress to get him out of debt. She had no intention of letting him touch her or her money.

"Good. Go pack a small bag, whatever you deem necessary to take today. We can send for your other belongings later," Liam instructed her. "Oh and Gemma, change your gown too. Something pretty, perhaps green to match your eyes."

"I'm to leave today? Isn't that sudden?"

Assuagement filled her at the idea of escaping Alfie. Her hand flew to her chest as she allowed herself to believe it was going to happen. Liam worked fast, not that she was complaining, but she thought it'd take more time for him to extract her from her cousin's clutches.

"Yes. I have a special license. We're to be married today."

"Give me fifteen minutes. I don't have a lot that needs to be packed immediately. I will instruct the housekeeper to pack the rest of my trunks for delivery to Marsden House."

"I will wait for you here. I need to have a private word with Alfie on how a woman in his care should be treated."

Liam's mouth crunched up into a firm line. Displeasure filled his eyes as he turned to pin Alfie with his gaze. They darkened to a stormy blue, one Gemma had never seen before. She wanted to tell Liam not to hurt her cousin for altruistic reasons, but if she were honest she wanted him beaten.

He would have forced himself on her if Liam hadn't walked in. Her skin still crawled with revulsion from the places he'd put his hands. She shuddered at the memory, disgusted she'd had to endure his groping. Gemma loathed the man as much as she adored Liam. They were two different men and each invoked a different feeling in her. Sadly, she wasn't at all happy with either emotion.

Living with unrequited love was horrible—dealing with Alfie's nasty disposition, however, was a far worse ordeal.

"Liam, don't hurt him—much." Gemma paused and waved her hand dismissively. "I'd hate for this to come back to haunt us."

He looked at her with a devilish smile. That carefree smile so full of sin had always been her undoing. Her heart skipped a beat, and her stomach started to tingle.

"Darling, I promise you he'll be hurting far more than it will show on the outside. He'll feel a pain that will haunt him long after we are gone from his life. Now scoot so I can inflict all those deep seated wounds he fully deserves."

Gemma nodded and ran out of the room. She skipped the steps and walked into her bedroom. She grabbed a valise and put a change of clothes in it. Then she took her jewelry case and a stack of letters. She placed them inside and tied it closed. Gemma didn't need much and everything necessary had been enclosed in the satchel. She found a green gown in her armoire and changed as fast as she could. Thankfully she followed Lily's advice and had had gowns made she could put on herself. She picked up the bag and with much haste went back to the sitting room.

She paused inside the doorway. Her eyes flew to Liam as he lounged on a nearby chair. His legs were crossed in an easy manner as he tapped restlessly on the arm. Alfie sat stiffly on the settee and held his stomach in a tight embrace. Not a mark showed anywhere on him as Liam had promised.

"I'm ready to go."

Liam turned and looked at her. He nodded in her direction and started to walk over to her side.

"You're both going to regret you've crossed me," Alfie spat out.

Liam stopped and turned back to Alfie before they exited the room.

"Alfie, don't do anything stupid." His voice was hard and commanding as he issued the reminder. "As long as you leave us be we will leave you alone. Make one wrong move towards me or Gemma and you will regret it. That isn't a threat. It's a promise. I take care of what's mine."

Gemma snorted. Liam had claimed her. She didn't believe he meant it. Whatever his reasons for helping her, it had nothing to do with wanting her. Still, a part of her couldn't help wishing it were true.

When she'd first heard the words, her whole body lit up with an uncontrollable longing.

Liam turned back to Gemma and placed her hand in the crook of his arm.

"Ready to go, love?" he asked, his tone softening just for her ears.

"Oh yes. Let's go and never look back."

She let him lead her out the door and to his awaiting carriage. Liam helped her as she entered the carriage and followed her inside. He took her bag and placed it under one of the seats and then sat across from her. The carriage started to move, and it jerked her forward causing her to collapse into his arms. She hadn't been prepared for it to depart.

"You always did fall into my arms." Liam laughed as he set her next to him on the seat.

"Don't go ruining a good rescue by turning into an arse," Gemma scolded him. "I know that was a farce. Did Lily put you up to it?"

"Not at all. Well, not entirely. She did ask for my father to help you out of the situation. He placed the particulars in my hands."

"And this is the solution you came up with?" Gemma paused with a sigh. "I'm sorry. I should be thanking you. Instead, I'm harping on how you did it."

She stared at him. "I don't mind really. It worked to get Alfie to let me go without a fight—well not much of one anyway. I truly do appreciate your assistance. I don't want to think about what he'd have done if you hadn't arrived in time." Gemma shuddered at the memory of her cousin's hands on her bosom. "I take it you are going to help me get to America so I can stay with your sister until I reach my majority?"

"No."

"What do you mean no?" she asked. "How am I going to escape from Alfie if I don't leave the country?"

"I thought that had already been settled. You're marrying me. Today. Nothing else is going to deter him."

"I don't want to marry you. I'd much rather go to South Carolina."

"We will do that. It is probably best we leave for a short period anyway. On our wedding trip can go visit Lily," he said.

"Why are you being obstinate? I am not going to marry you."

"Yes, you are." Liam emphasized each word as he looked her directly in the eyes. Gemma's lips pursed, disbelief filling her as he spoke. "Your father gave his

DAWN BROWER

permission. You are stuck with me. You just told Alfie you didn't want to refuse me."

Were they actually getting married? The infernal flutter of hope sprung to life. Gemma didn't know if she could eradicate it again. Did her father truly want her to marry Liam? She bit her lip and once again wished he was still around to ask. He'd know what to do. But if the contract Liam had was legit, it was clear her father had wanted her to marry him. She already had her answer.

Warmth pooled in her cheeks. She clenched her fists in her lap.

Gemma wanted to scream with outrage. Damn her rotten luck. She knew Liam didn't love her, and she didn't want to find herself stuck in a loveless marriage. Worse yet he knew she loved him once; maybe he counted on her still having those feelings for him. No matter what she said, she was far from over him. A one-sided love—married to him for the rest of her life—would be hell. She had to make him see that it wouldn't work.

"Can't we just pretend?" Gemma asked. "You don't want to marry me, Liam. Don't make me hate you."

"You are not going to talk me out of this, Gemma.

It's decided. I've accepted it, and now you need to as well."

"Like hell I do,"

Gemma pushed him back and scooted across to the other side of the carriage. She didn't need to sit next to him while he dictated to her.

"No need to make things interesting, love. I'm already willing. Now sit back and relax. The rector is expecting us to arrive shortly."

"What rector?"

"The one in the next town. I've made all the arrangements. I already told you I had a special license, didn't I," he said. "In less than an hour you will be my wife. Don't worry you'll get used to the idea.

If Gemma had something to throw at him, it would have already bounced off his head. Liam Marsden had to be the most stubborn male in existence.

"Bloody hell, you are irritating."

"Welcome to my world," he said with a droll smile. "It's all part of the plan, love. Makes life more… intriguing."

Gemma sat back in her seat and fumed. Winning an argument with Liam was akin to dreams becoming reality. No way would he allow her to get ahead. Just like the real world never compared to the bliss of dreams.

Neither one had a chance of happening for her right now. She gave up on her fantasies a long time ago; just as she now gave up on convincing Liam to forego marrying her. It would amount to wasted energy and useless hope.

Gemma knew when to sit back and lick her wounds to fight another day. If she had to be Liam's wife, she'd need a new plan of attack. She had learned from the best and Lily had taught her well. Her fiancé didn't know what he had in store for him.

Gemma didn't give up anything that belonged to her.

Liam would love her or at the very least desire her as much as she did him. With a plan forming in her head, she relaxed, and her lips lifted into a half smile.

CHAPTER THREE

Things hadn't gone quite as Liam had planned it. The situation had gotten out of control when he walked in and saw Alfie's hands all over Gemma. Rage filled him as he fought to restrain himself from murdering the rotten bastard.

How dare he force himself on a woman!

Seeing Gemma fighting off his unwanted attentions had changed his approach to the situation. He had come in prepared for anything, but hoping for the best. Marriage to Gemma was only to be utilized as a last resort. She had been right in assuming the contract was a means to extricate her from her cousins clutches. Liam never thought he'd be grateful for his father's foresight. For once the unwanted betrothal with Lord Devon appeared to be a good thing.

When he'd first heard about it years ago, he'd been angry and disillusioned. So much so he'd listened to his sister's scheme and along with her and his best friend, Noah, he had run away. How serendipitous his father still had the original contract. If Lord Devon hadn't insisted on his father keeping it, they wouldn't have had the means to extricate Lady Gemma from Alfie's clutches.

Now he found himself on the way to his own wedding.

Sweat beaded on his forehead. He wiped it away with the back of his hand. A flutter of energy dissipated throughout his stomach. Oh hell, he was getting married and soon. What had he gotten himself into?

Liam originally had no intention of going through with the ceremony. Tying himself to one woman was the last thing he wanted at that point in his life. He was too bloody young to even consider the idea. He couldn't back out of the situation now. Fate had decided on a new path for him, and it included Gemma as his wife.

The carriage rolled to a stop in front of a vicarage. Liam leaned forward and looked out the window. He glanced at his bride-to-be and found her to be sitting calming across from him. At least she had stopped arguing with him. Thank goodness for small favors, he didn't want to drag an unwilling bride into the vicarage. What would the vicar think then? How would he explain it? Gemma had to be willing, or it wouldn't work.

"Wait here. I'm going to see if they are ready for us. I will retrieve you once it's time to start the ceremony," he told her.

"Fine."

"You're not going to argue with me?" he asked.

Thank God. The last thing he needed was to fight with Gemma before the wedding. The one he hadn't set up yet. He didn't want her to realize how much he'd been bluffing since he'd walked into the sitting room and found Alfie attacking her.

The urge to protect Gemma became ingrained in his soul in an instant.

Gemma always bickered with him and now wouldn't be a good time for her to unleash her inner wrath. He had come to accept it as second nature for her, but for this to work she needed to project a calm demeanor.

"No point."

Gemma had to be plotting something. Liam

knew her too well to believe anything else. His twin sister, Lily, happened to be the queen of devious plans. No doubt she had taught her best friend how to create the most intricate ones. He needed to be at his best if he hoped to thwart whatever rambled through her brain.

"All right. I will be back shortly," he told her as he stepped out of the carriage.

He ambled inside the vicarage and found the clergyman sitting at one of the pews near the altar, his head bent down in prayer. The man obviously hadn't heard Liam walk inside as he only looked up once he stood in next to him.

"Sorry to disturb you," Liam said. "I had hoped you could perform a wedding today."

"Yours I assume?" the vicar asked.

"Yes. I'd like to get married immediately. My fiancée awaits your decision in the carriage."

"I presume you have a special license as the bans have not been read in this vicarage."

"Indeed I do. Will you perform the ceremony?" Liam asked.

"I will as long as you are both willing."

He hoped Gemma wouldn't make a fuss. This was for her own good. If he was willing, she better damn well be too.

"We are."

"Very well, retrieve your young woman. I will perform the ceremony."

Liam nodded and strolled out of the vicarage. Now to get Gemma inside so they could get married without any unforeseen interruptions. He hadn't planned on a wedding that day, but at least everything seemed to be falling into place. She didn't need to know exactly what his original intentions were though. Liam hadn't wanted to marry her, but he'd been left with no choice. Alfie would never leave her alone if she remained unwed.

He'd always stand by her, and that's all the information Gemma would need to know. That included tying them together forever. He just accepted them as a fact. Gemma needed him therefore he gave her the only thing that would help... himself and everything it entailed.

"It's time Gemma. Follow me inside," he said as he opened the carriage door.

"Do we really need to take it this far?"

"We are not going to go over this again, Gemma. Come inside."

She reached out and grabbed onto his hand for support as she exited the carriage. Her gloved hand slid across his palm leaving a trail of heat. Once her feet hit the ground, she looked back up into his eyes, her jade green eyes staring back at him in defiance.

Liam sighed. She didn't appear too happy at the prospect of being his wife. Too bloody bad—this wasn't an ideal situation in his eyes either.

"If this is my only choice I will make the best of it. Rest assured I do know when to give in and fight another day. I just wanted to make sure that you are positive you want to tie yourself to me forever. I know how you feel about me," she said.

"You have no idea what I feel for you Gemma. You never did. Let's go attend our wedding now. The vicar is patiently waiting for us."

Gemma followed him inside making small steps ensuring a slow progress. Liam could feel his pulse start to race with anticipation. Heat spread through him. Desire he'd never experienced before. A thousand sensations traveled over him leaving him breathless. Soon he would be her husband, but something even more surprising became evident to him.

In a short time, Gemma would be his.

It was simultaneously enlightening and terrifying. He started to shake with the sudden realization —Gemma would soon be his wife. This was truly and utterly happening. She would belong solely to him and no one else. He would have a claim on her that he never realized he wanted. Somehow that made all the difference to him as he turned and waited with extreme patience for her to join him in front of the vicar.

"I know it's been a taxing day love, but we have an even longer journey back to London," he said with an amused smile. "But I'm a patient man. I'm willing to wait forever to make you mine."

"I know exactly how patient you are Liam. Trust me when I say my fervor matches yours."

"Good. Then we can proceed at a quicker pace. Vicar whenever you wish to begin we are ready," Liam said.

"I am ready now. Please join me here," the vicar said.

They ambled over to join him. The vicar started the ceremony and for Liam it went by in a blur. He barely remembered saying the vows which joined him and Gemma together. Through the entire ceremony, he stared into her green eyes and lost himself in their depths. Something lurked there, something that he hadn't noticed before. He couldn't explain it, but he felt he had missed an important detail. A facet that made Gemma essential to him, but he couldn't pinpoint the exact element that had changed. Maybe the only real change resided deep inside him. Perhaps Gemma had not changed at all, but how he saw her had.

"You are now man and wife," the vicar said. "You may now kiss your bride."

Liam looked up at the vicar startled at his pronouncement.

"What?"

"Never mind Liam," Gemma said with a disgusted voice. "You don't need to kiss me. We have a long journey ahead. We should go. Thank you again, vicar for marrying us."

Gemma started to leave, but Liam stopped her. He turned her to face him, and he could see how much he had disappointed her. She wanted to kiss him, and he had ruined the moment by being lost in his own thoughts. How could he be so foolish? The least he could do was make this day as happy as possible for her. It wasn't and ideal situation. They should get some enjoyment from their wedding. His heart thrummed hard in his chest and sweat dripped down his neck.

In that instant he realized he wanted to kiss her too.

"I want to kiss my wife."

He leaned down and pressed his lips against hers.

With as much gentleness as he could muster Liam placed a soft kiss on her lips; with a slow pace he caressed them with his own over and over again. He pulled her into his arms and with gentle hands stroked her back. She let out a small breath of satisfaction.

Liam wanted more, and he promised himself he would have it later. The first taste of her lips left him with a craving like none before. He pulled back and saw his own need reflected in her eyes. They had that at least. An equal desire for each other, but Liam knew he couldn't press her just yet.

If their marriage was to have any chance of becoming anything good, they had to take their time with each other. They had the rest of their lives together. He wasn't sure if it was a good thing or a bad thing, but he looked forward to learning everything he could about his new wife.

"Let's go home, Lady Marsden."

"I don't think I'll get used to that anytime soon," she said.

"You will. Sooner than you realize."

"What's next Liam?"

"Other than going home? We will plan a trip to visit my sister in America. I want to meet my new nephew, and she will want to make sure you are all right. We won't leave right away though. I have some things to take care of before we can make the trip."

Liam nodded at the vicar as they walked out faster than they had come in. They really did have a long journey ahead of them. It would be at least an hour before they made it back to London. He didn't want to waste any time lingering in the church. He helped Gemma back into the carriage, and he settled once again across from her.

"How long do you think before we leave?"

"Two weeks at least, if I can manage to get everything in place that quick. A month at most," he said. "Are you in a hurry to share a small space with me?"

"Not at all. My urgency is a deep desire to see Lily again. It has been three years since she left. I miss her terribly. I too want to meet her new son."

"And you shall. I promise."

"Because you always keep your promises?" she asked with sarcasm as she leaned her head against the side of the carriage.

She might not believe he did, but she'd learn soon enough. Liam was as good on his word. Once given, he made sure he didn't disappoint the person he'd given it to.

"I do indeed, Gemma. Every last one of them," he

said with desire in his eyes. "One day you will know exactly how good I am at keeping a promise."

"I think I already know," her voice just above a whisper. "I don't need any demonstrations."

"Don't worry, love. I don't plan on giving one anytime soon. Relax we have a while before we arrive home."

She looked at him and turned her head to look out the window. Her choice not to answer him told him everything she tried to hide. He knew her desire as well as he knew his own. Two years ago she had let him know exactly how much she wanted him. He had turned her away then. A mistake, he knew it now. She didn't fully trust him, but he would rectify that with time. Soon she would see that she could rely on him for anything.

CHAPTER FOUR

Gemma sat in silence for the rest of the trip to London. She still had trouble wrapping her mind around the fact that she had just married Liam Marsden. Saying yes had really only been a token effort on her part; marrying him had always been her secret wish. Perhaps not the wisest choice she had ever made, but she knew that she couldn't turn back and change it. Marriages were not as easily undone as they were to enter into. She only hoped that she wouldn't come to regret her choice. No matter what Liam said, she knew he wouldn't have forced her into the marriage if she had truly been adamant against it. She looked out the window of the carriage and saw the outskirts of London coming into view.

"Not much longer and we will be at our destination."

Liam looked over at her. He had been quiet for the rest of the journey as well. Gemma couldn't help but wonder what he had rolling through his mind. She wished she knew why he insisted marriage was their only option.

"True enough, I'm sure you are as ready to get out of this carriage as I am," he said.

"Probably more so, on your part. You did travel more than I have today."

"More than you know."

"What do you mean?" she asked.

Maybe if she got him to talk a little bit she'd figure out what his plan was. Liam had a way of being closed mouthed. Gemma didn't understand what was going on, but at least she could be thankful to be out of her cousin's clutches. Even if Liam irritated her, Gemma knew she owed him more than she could ever pay back.

"It's nothing. Suffice to say I had a lot to accomplish in a short time."

"You're not going to tell me are you?" Gemma pursed her lips in displeasure.

"I don't see the point," he said, frustrated. "I'm tired Gemma. Just leave it be."

Liam wouldn't discuss it with her even if he didn't have the excuse of being tired. She wouldn't push the issue... yet. She knew when to let something go and bring it back up at a later time. He may not want to answer her questions now, but he would when she was ready to force him to.

"Fine."

"You're not going to try to make me talk? That's a refreshing change," Liam said.

"I'm in a semi-good mood. Don't ruin it by being an imbecile." Gemma glared at him.

"I'm never without wit, love."

"Truly?" she raised her eyebrow in question. "You could have fooled me."

"Now who's being the difficult one?" he asked with an amused laugh.

"I call it as I see it, *love.*" She emphasized the last word with sarcasm. Gemma believed he mocked her by saying it so offhanded when talking to her. He didn't love her, and she didn't see the point of the charade.

"Do you now?" he asked. A cocky grin filled his handsome face."Should make our lives inherently more interesting."

"Absolutely." Wickedness filled her, and she grinned up at him, letting it shine through.

Maybe she should look at this as an opportunity. One she could use to her advantage. She'd have more freedom as a married woman. As she studied Liam, she realized something else.

He was her husband.

By marrying her, he'd give her the right to take certain liberties—with him. Part of her was rather excited at the prospect. A tingle of energy fluttered inside of her. Yes, maybe this marriage thing wouldn't be so bad.

"I don't like that look on you. Whatever idea you just formed I'd advise against it."

Liam had no idea. Gemma wasn't the meek wall-flower he first met. She'd had to grow up and fast. Her father's death changed everything for her. Losing him—dealing with her awful cousin—it gave her the backbone she'd been lacking before. Her husband had no idea how much courage it had taken her to tell him how she felt about him two years ago. Loving Liam made her brave. Too bad he never returned her feelings. Now he was hers and she'd find a way to make him pay for that slight, without losing her heart to him again.

"Of course you would. I happen to think it's a rather genius idea."

"Gemma..."

"What?" Innocence resonated through her voice.

"Nothing. I'm not going to humor you with a response. I'm going back to my own corner and enjoy the peace and quiet."

"Coward." Gemma ground her bottom lip between her teeth and raised an eyebrow. She licked the sting from her lip and then asked, "Are you afraid of little ole' me?"

He gave her a scathing look. Some things just didn't change. Liam had always been so easy for her to goad into a response. He failed to realize she only wanted his attention. Something he didn't usually deign to give her. Which is why the marriage had come as a shock to her, Liam usually avoided her. The carriage came to a stop and surprised Gemma. She looked out and saw a townhouse she didn't recognize.

"This isn't Marsden House."

"Of course not, Marsden's my parents' home," Liam said.

"I didn't realize you had your own townhouse."

"No reason you would. I haven't had it that long, and we haven't socialized in a while," he said. "Come let's go inside. They are expecting us."

He'd certainly thought of everything. The staff probably had everything arranged for his new wife's arrival. Too bad she'd not been given the luxury of being prepared.

Liam stepped out of the carriage and turned to help her down. She took his hand and jumped down. He continued to hold onto her as he escorted her inside her new home where the staff greeted them.

"This is the butler, Pemberly and the house-keeper, Janie." Liam introduced them. "This is my wife, Lady Marsden."

"Welcome home," they both said in unison.

"Is Lady Marsden's room ready?" Liam asked.

"Yes, sir it is," Janie said.

"Good. Can you show her around the house and where her room will be?" Liam asked.

"You're not going to show me around?" Gemma asked.

"No, I have some things to do."

She couldn't believe he was leaving her. Alone. In a new home she'd never laid eyes on before. How inconsiderate...

"I thought you just said you were tired," Gemma said with a petulant voice.

"I am," Liam rubbed his temples in frustration. "Don't be difficult Gemma."

Her husband was an arse. How dare he tell her not to be difficult? She had every right to be as demanding as she wanted. Her whole life had been uprooted, and while it was a good thing it was still rather drastic. Why couldn't he understand how unsettled it all had made her? Did the blasted man every really look at anything around him? Gemma didn't see the point in arguing with him. If he wanted to abandon her she'd let him. This was her life now. She'd just have to find a way to get through her husband's tough shell. It would just take time. For now, though, she didn't want to lay eyes on him. His actions disgusted her and she had more pride than to beg.

"I see. So you are going to run away already. I'm not surprised. Will I see you later?"

"No. I will be out."

"Ah. I get it. Go run to your club, Liam. I'll be fine here with Janie and Pemberly. I don't need you." Gemma turned to walk towards Janie.

Damn her infernal heart—why did she allow herself to start to hope. She *knew* better.

"Gemma, wait..."

No doubt he had a list of reasons why he needed to leave. She didn't have the energy or inclination to listen to him droll on about them. She'd rather he go and save herself the aggravation.

"Go, Liam. I see you have more pressing—issues."

She turned her attention to the butler and housekeeper.

"Now, Janie, I'd love a tour. Please show me around my new home," Gemma said with as much enthusiasm she could muster. She'd been taking care of herself for a while now—since her father passed away. A sharp pain stabbed through her chest as she remembered the loss. "Pemberly, could you please see to it that my satchel is taken to my room. I believe it's still in the carriage."

"Yes, Lady Marsden," Pemberly said and turned to leave the room.

Gemma turned to see Liam still standing in the entryway. His lips were twitching downward. Eyes narrowed to tiny slits he observed her with the staff. His arms were folded across his chest, his head slightly tilted, as he tapped his foot. If Gemma were to hazard a guess, he seemed to be contemplating what his next move would be.

"Why are you still here?" she asked. "I thought you had something better to do."

"It isn't like that, Gemma."

"It never is, is it?"

"I don't understand why you are so damned angry, but I'm not going to sit here and have a disagreement with you in front of the servants. We will discuss this later."

"Fine by me."

Gemma watched as Liam stormed out of the house. She fought tears from falling down her face. None of it should surprise her. He only married her to protect her from her awful cousin. He never promised or claimed to love her. She couldn't hold him responsible for her broken heart. No, she knew where to place the blame; it belonged squarely on her shoulders.

She foolishly still loved Liam Marsden. Stupid of her to hope he might return those feelings... No time to cry, there were other more pressing matters at hand. She had a household to get familiar with and servants waiting for her direction.

"Janie, please show me around the house."

"It would be my pleasure, Lady Marsden," Janie said.

Janie led her around and showed her every nook and cranny. The townhouse was lovely and bright. It would be a wonderful place to live and raise a family. If only she thought a family might be in her future. Maybe someday, if her husband ever touched her again. That kiss in the church had to be an anomaly.

"This here is your room. It was prepared for you earlier today."

"And where is my husband's room?"

"Right next door."

"Thank you, Janie," Gemma said. "I think I am going to retire to the sitting room. Can you have tea sent there?"

"Absolutely madam. Would you like something to eat as well?"

"Yes, something light. It's been a long day, and I don't want a heavy meal. I don't want supper tonight."

"Very well, I will have it prepared."

Janie left her standing in her bedroom. The coloring matched her eyes. The draperies and bedspread were both a nice shade of green. She had to wonder if Liam had ordered the room made up in that color or if it had already been decorated in that shade. He had asked her to change into a green gown earlier. It made her wonder how much he noticed about her.

How silly of her to consider he'd made the room up in a color to match her eyes. He wouldn't have gone that far. It would imply he'd been planning this for a while. Gemma knew that couldn't have been possible. It was only her wishful thinking that Liam might have feelings for her beyond protecting her from Alfie.

Speculating about the possible motivations of her husband wouldn't get her anywhere. She already had a sharp sting in her chest. No need to add to the pain. She walked out of the room and down the stairs. She weaved her way through the hallway until she located the sitting room. She sat down and waited for her tea to arrive.

"Excuse me, Lady Marsden," Pemberly said. "I know you just arrived, but we have a caller."

"We do? Who?"

"That would be me," a male voice said.

Gemma looked up into the eyes of a very handsome man. She had never seen him before, but if she had he might have given Liam a rival for her attention. Never before had she seen such a good-looking man. His features were as dark as Liam's were light. The shade of his hair held the hue of a black midnight sky and his eyes a deep rich brown, like chocolate. His countenance screamed power and authority. This man was not someone to toil with.

"I don't know you," she said. "I'm sorry, that's rather rude of me."

"No apologies necessary," he said smoothly. "I don't socialize so you wouldn't know me on sight.

You probably recognize my name though. I am Noah St. John, Duke of Huntly."

"Oh, now I certainly feel more foolish, Your Grace. I have to ask though why are you here?"

"I came to see your husband, Liam."

"Oh, Pemberly probably told you he isn't in. He left rather suddenly."

"He did indeed, but when he said Lady Marsden was in I had to meet you."

"Oh, and why?"

"Because I didn't believe my dear friend had succumbed to marriage when he vowed he wouldn't for many years to come. His new wife had to be an enchantress of some sort. It's my duty as his friend to see for myself that he made a good choice." He grinned. "You're quite beautiful, Lady Marsden. Liam is a lucky man. You sure you want to stay with him?"

Gemma didn't know if she should be flattered or appalled. Did Liam put him up to this nonsense? She didn't think he had a cruel bone in his body, but she had been wrong before.

"What are you after, Your Grace?"

"I don't know what you mean."

"Why are you throwing flattery at me and asking me so blatantly if I want to leave my husband... of less than five hours."

"So the newness hasn't worn off yet?" The duke raised his eyebrow, mocking her.

Ah, she understood now. The duke was a rake and ascertaining her intentions. She didn't believe in being unfaithful and wouldn't find a lover to replace her husband. Liam was the only one she ever truly wanted. Besides, she had no clue what true passion entailed. She didn't know what she missed by denying herself the joys of intimacy.

The Duke of Huntly wouldn't be getting anywhere with her. Even if Liam never truly loved her, nothing would get her to be untrue to herself. When she made a vow, she meant it and had every intention of keeping it. Even in the face of such a handsome, enticing male, she would stay true to her beliefs.

"You're cynical. That's your problem. You don't believe anyone can be faithful to each other. I get it now. You're testing me. Rest assured, Your Grace, I don't plan on having an affair with anyone." Moisture formed on her palms. Gemma wiped them across her skirts. "If that is all you came to ascertain, you can turn around and leave. It's been a trying day, and I'd rather not deal with anymore… difficulties."

"No one ever does, dear. Look at you. Liam left

you all alone on your wedding night, no less. It won't take long for your bed to be too cold, and you'll want someone to warm it up for you." His lips tilted up into a cocky smile. "Let me know if you change your mind and I'll be happy to show you what true pleasure is."

An unladylike snort erupted from her mouth. She tilted her head and looked closely at the duke. His eyes had narrowed into tiny slits, and his lips curled into a sensuous smile. His arms were folded across his chest. True pleasure he said. Gemma didn't doubt he could deliver on that promise. If only Liam had been the one to offer it to her, then she'd have been already leaping into his arms. This man would never do though.

"How kind of you to offer yourself to service my needs," she said with derision in her voice. "I'm going to have to decline your very generous offer, Your Grace. I'm not into inflicting pain on myself. Besides, I respect myself too much. I'm sure you won't have any trouble finding a different candidate."

"Indeed I won't. I'm not used to getting turned down," he said. His lips tilted into a half smile filled with cockiness.

"You proposition the wives' of your friends'

often?" Gemma asked, sarcasm laced through her voice.

"No." The Duke of Huntly laughed. "Only you hold that distinction. I had to be sure, you see."

"So you wouldn't have become my lover if I jumped at the chance?" Gemma raised her eyebrow questioningly.

She could see the play of emotions on his face. This man before her was a conundrum. She didn't understand him completely. Gemma wasn't even sure how close his relationship was to her husband. Why did he come in and immediately proposition her? What kind of game was he playing with her? Gemma didn't like playing the fool and didn't appreciate this man making her look and feel silly.

"On the contrary, I would have, if only to prove to Liam exactly what kind of woman he married," he said quietly.

"I see, so you did this all for purely altruistic intentions," she said with skepticism in her voice. "Somehow I doubt that."

"Very astute of you. I promise I won't ever offer again. I honestly am only looking out for Liam."

"A little late don't you think? We *are* already married."

"Nothing is ever too late." He shook his head.

"Something could have been done to correct the mistake."

"Really? What possible solutions would you have for it?" she asked.

"Annulment, if possible... divorce, if not. Death is usually final."Her mouth hung open for several seconds as she processed his word. Once she got control over her thoughts, she stared up into his brown depths. "Death? Really? That's a bit extreme, isn't it?" Surely he didn't mean what he insinuated.

"Yes. Quite so. Sometimes it doesn't give us much of a choice." A solemn glint in his eyes as grief filled his voice. "Death waits for no one."

Noah St. John had some dark stains on his soul. She could see shadows in his eyes telling her he had ingrained demons buried inside him compounded by unearthly pain. Gemma didn't want to dig too deep for fear of what she'd find. It also became clear that he had no idea how to relate to anyone. Someone had hurt him, and he carried the wounds around for the world to see. She didn't know what happened to him, but her heart hurt just looking at the grave look in his chocolate-brown eyes.

"I don't think I want to know why you feel that way, Your Grace. It's been a long day, and I'm going to retire soon. Do you wish to leave a message for my husband?"

"No. I will stop by again another day and catch up with him." He nodded and added, "You're different. I think I like you. Someday I will figure out where you got that backbone of steel. For now I bid you goodnight."

The duke turned to leave. Gemma watched him walk out the door. After he left, Janie pushed in a cart with tea and a light repast. She sat down on the settee and poured a cup of tea. Absentminded she sipped it as she pondered the odd conversation she had with the duke. Then, she shook her head. She didn't see the point in worrying about the Duke of Huntly. She had more pressing concerns, like how to deal with her husband.

CHAPTER FIVE

*L*iam had intended to visit his father to give him an update on the situation. Gemma's attitude had him going to his club instead, exactly as she had suggested. Her claws had come out, and she had assumed the worst in him. He tried to explain to her that he needed to see his father, but she kept pushing him away. No one could drive him mad faster than Gemma. She had always been able to make him angrier than anyone else. He took a swig of brandy and set the glass down on the table. What he should do is go home and make love to his new wife, but he had already decided he needed to wait. They didn't have a normal romance or courtship. Liam believed they needed time to adjust before taking that step.

"Met your wife earlier this evening."

Liam looked up at his best friend, Noah, and smiled.

"I see you survived relatively intact, Gemma must be having an off night." The smile left Liam's face to be replaced with a grimace as he regarded his friend. He picked up his glass of brandy and downed the remaining liquid. It burned as it traveled down his throat. His head shook in several involuntary rapid successions.

"That bad?" Noah let out a loud whistle and sat down. He grinned down at Liam and raised his eyebrow. "I found her rather charming."

"She has her moments." Liam ran his finger around the rim of his empty glass. He needed more brandy."Unfortunately I don't get to see them very often."

"Why the hell did you marry her if she's such a harridan?"

"I don't know. I didn't plan it. I just needed to." How do you explain the loss of your mind? That was the only explanation for marrying Gemma. He was only supposed to use the contract as a means of extricating her. Instead, he'd been compelled to marry her. Damned if he understood why. Deep down he believed he'd made the right decision, even if it didn't feel like it was. "I know that doesn't make sense. I can't wrap my head around it myself."

"I admit I was a bit confused to find her in your house. The same chit your father attempted to betroth you to when we were still at Eton. It boggled my mind—thought there might be something nefarious afoot. What gives?"

"Yeah, I never thought I'd marry her either." Liam paused, tilted his head, and considered how to explain it to his best friend. "When I saw her, Alfie had his hand down her dress—I saw red. She drives me insane, but no woman should have to put up with something so bloody awful."

"Bloody hell. You're in love with her," Noah said, shock filling his voice.

Liam's breath seized inside his chest. No, he didn't—couldn't love Gemma. He only married her to protect her. Nothing more...

"Of course not. Don't be absurd. I don't love her. I..."

Noah raised his eyebrow at him with a questioning look in his eyes. No way, no how. Liam did not love Gemma, did he? He had strong feelings for her whenever he found himself in her company. He had simply chalked that up to them disliking each other. What had his father said about it being a different form of passion? Could both his father and Noah be right?

"No, I don't love her," he reiterated. "I'm not sure I even like her."

"Is that why you are here getting drunk?"

Liam nodded. "She got all mad because I had to leave. Acted like I was abandoning her. I was only going to go see my father. He needed to know what happened."

"So you left your blushing bride to go visit your father?" Noah asked. "It couldn't have waited until the next day?"

Put like that, Liam could see why Gemma had reacted the way she had. He shouldn't have even planned to leave her alone. No reason his father couldn't have waited until the next day to hear the news.

Liam wondered if he'd be surprised that he married Gemma after all.

His father seemed to believe that strong feelings existed between him and his new wife. The blasted man probably would laugh, thinking he was right.Liam would have to disabuse him of that notion rather quickly. The last thing he needed to hear was his father's gloating. He would make sure not to mention how he blundered when he brought her home. His father had a strange sense of humor and would find his predicament hilarious.

"You're right. I messed up. Clearly I've lost my mind and I'm not thinking straight," Liam said in a remorseful voice.

"Damn right, I am." Noah picked up his glass of brandy and took a drink."By and by. She's a spitfire that wife of yours."

"Why do you say that? Did you do something to make her even more livid?" Liam asked. "I've already got to atone for my own blunder, please tell me you didn't make it worse."

"I may have." Noah nodded, guilt filling his eyes. "I couldn't understand why you got married so fast. I expected a cloying manipulative female. Your wife didn't appreciate my methods of determining her worth."

"Oh hell, what did you do?"

If Noah messed things up even worse... Liam would be paying for a long time. He already blundered all on his own. He didn't need his friends adding onto the situation. Gemma wasn't likely to forgive him for some time. Bloody hell.

"Not much. Not nearly as much as I could have done," Noah explained. "I only propositioned her a bit. She didn't take the bait though. I'm not sure she likes me after my blatant innuendos."

If Liam hadn't already downed a bottle of brandy, he'd consider starting another one. No, what he should do is punch Noah in the face for even thinking of issuing his wife an unsavory invitation. Liam fumbled forward and almost fell out of his chair. Gripping the table he pushed himself back and leaned against his chair. He clenched his fists together as heat traveled up the back of his neck. Noah's idiotic actions were sure to cause him more trouble once he got home.

"Damn it, Noah. Gemma isn't like the females you know. She is innocent."

"I know that now." He shrugged his shoulders. "I didn't then, nothing to do about it now. I'm glad she's one of the good ones. You deserve to be happy."

Time would tell—Liam had his doubts about happiness with Gemma. They might find a certain level of it, but they'd probably fall short of finding true bliss.

"So do you. Don't discount finding someone to love again."

"Marriage isn't for me. I've already tried that route, and it left me devastated. I'm not about to open myself to that kind of pain again."

"I know you feel that no other female can compare to Rubina. You loved her, but she's gone. Don't let her death ruin your life."

"It's not as simple as that. I never told you how we argued that day." Noah's face grew dark, and sadness permeated his eyes. His eyes scanned the room never fully looking at Liam. "She left because she needed a break from me. She told me that I was too intense for her, and she couldn't be my everything. I needed to find a way to live without her. She got her bloody wish. The only problem is I'm merely surviving, without her I've always been a little lost. I don't want another wife. There's no way I'll put a female through the tragedy of getting too close to me."

"You might change your mind someday," Liam said, "I hope you do. I'd like my friend to be happy again."

"I doubt it. I'm not meant to have a family. You get rather used to being alone when your parents die when you're still a child." Noah said. "But that isn't the issue right now. We need to figure out how to get back into your wife's good graces."

"Gemma doesn't hold a grudge. She'll forgive you." Liam shook his head, disgusted with himself. "Me, on the other hand, she will make grovel. This isn't the first time we've had a disagreement. We tend to quarrel a lot."

"That's another form of heat between you. Just channel it in another way. She'll forgive you."

"Of course she will, eventually," Liam said. "I'm not sure she'll accept me in her bed just yet. We had a rather unusual courtship. By that I mean we haven't had one at all."

"How did you end up married to Lady Gemma of all women? Last I knew you didn't intend to get married any time soon."

"That I didn't. It's Lily's fault."

"What does your sister have to do with it?" Noah asked baffled.

"Gemma is her friend. Lily wrote Father asking him to help her. Gemma's cousin, Alfie, intended to force her to marry him so he could get his hands on her money."

"So your father made you marry her?"

"No, he'd never insist on that. He learned his lesson about forcing one of us to marry against our will a long time ago, as you know." Liam took another swig of his brandy. "He suggested two options. Marriage only if I cared for the girl. I had every intention of going through with the other plan until I saw Alfie attacking Gemma. I jumped in and claimed her before I knew what I was doing."

"Marrying her was your first instinct?" Noah asked.

"Yes, and pummeling my fists into Alfie as soon as she left the room."

"Now that makes a bit more sense. That's the Liam I know." Noah's laugh echoed through the room.

"He deserved it. When I walked in, I found him groping her, and the bodice of her dress ripped."

"I'm sure he did deserve it. I'm not arguing with you. I applaud your restraint. I may have murdered him myself."

"If he ever comes near Gemma again I might do that."

Liam didn't like the idea of anyone ever touching his wife. He would commit murder in order to protect her. She didn't know exactly what he was capable of, but she should. When he told her he took care of what belonged to him, he meant it.

Someone came by and refilled his glass. He picked it up and swished the contents around. The aroma filled his nose, enticing him; he tipped it back and drank it in one swig. This time the burn made him feel good as it traveled down his throat. He set the empty tumbler down on the table and stood up. The room spun around a bit, and he grabbed onto his chair for support.

"You should go home to your wife. It's getting late. Do you need help getting home?"

"I'm only slightly foxed. I think I can manage to get home on my own." Liam tilted backward a bit. He held out his arms to steady himself. Who the hell made the room spin?

"Right. I can see how capable you are. Come on, I'll give you a lift in my carriage."

"All right. I think that perhaps you're right."

"I'm always right." Noah reminded him as he helped him up.

Noah stood up next to Liam, and they left the club. Liam's stumbled forward in a haze as he followed his friend to his carriage. He climbed inside and fell in a clumsy heap on one of the seats. Noah motioned for the driver to start moving, and the slow rock of the carriage made Liam's stomach churned with each rotation.

"You're not going to be sick, are you?"

"I must be looking pretty green for you to be asking me that," Liam said. "I'm fine. Just a little dizzy."

He could see the skepticism in Noah's eyes, but

he told the truth. He didn't feel sick at all. Simply disoriented.

"You do look like hell. I haven't seen you drink this much in a very long time. I suppose you picked a good time to get seriously inebriated. Marriage does that to a man. Throws us all off balance."

"Right. Probably shouldn't have married her. Thanks for pointing that out to me," Liam said with a lot of sarcasm. "Don't really regret it though, don't know why."

"Maybe you should figure out why. It might be an important detail you're suppressing."

Gemma once told him she loved him. What were the chances she still did? How would that play a part in their marriage? Liam's heart beat hard inside his chest. His breathing became more rapid. He rubbed his hand over the ache beneath his ribs—something was wrong with him.

Did he want Gemma to still be in love with him?

Surely she'd have given up on that girlish wish. What would he do if she hadn't stopped loving him? Could he learn to love her? Perhaps he could...

Liam knew one thing for certain, he needed to court his wife. Not tonight though, his drunken state was less than desirable. He had one final thought right before he passed out cold. It's a good thing he didn't intend on making love to Gemma once he made it home. He would be a dismal failure as a lover, and she deserved a special night.

Liam couldn't give it to her, so they would have to put off their wedding night—he was a bloody fool.

CHAPTER SIX

*G*emma had heard her husband come in late. The constant fumbling and failed attempt at a quiet murmur woke her up. She didn't know who had helped him to his bed and did not care.

The fact that someone had to assist him told her all she needed to know.

Liam had decided to carouse with friends and get inebriated instead of spending time with her. His actions caused a feeling of deep hurt and betrayal; the pain threatened to swallow her whole.

After a short time, the door next to hers opened and closed with a muffled thud. Soft footsteps could be heard in the hallway as they passed by her bedroom door, indicating that her husband's rescuer had left. Gemma had no desire to see who had aided Liam, but she did have an overwhelming need to talk with her foolish husband.

She got up out of bed and donned her wrapper. Crossing the room she opened the door and took slow, silent steps towards the bedroom next to hers. Stopping in front of the closed door she started to doubt the wisdom of visiting her husband's room.

Did she really want to go in there?

Yes, she did—Liam needed to know what a nitwit he was. She opened the door and walked inside before she changed her mind. Light from the moon streamed through the room and gave it an eerie glow. On tiptoes, she moved with as much stealth as she could manage over to the bed where she saw Liam's body spread in a haphazard fashion across its vast space.

The bed, a rumpled mess, much like the clothes still hanging on Liam's lax body, gave the impression of chaos. The person who had brought him home had simply dumped him on the bed. One boot stood on the floor next to the bed, the other on its side in front of the bedside table.

"Liam," she whispered. When he didn't answer she said in a louder more firm voice, "Liam, wake up."

"Hmm—what—Gemma?"

"Good, you're awake I want to discuss something with you."

"Not a good time." His voice still held the remnants of his drunken escapade. He slurred over his words, but Gemma didn't care. She had something to say and intended to say it whether he liked it or not.

"I'm not happy, Liam. I don't think we should have gotten married. If you hadn't been so adamant, I wouldn't have done it. I love you, but I don't want to be married to a man who doesn't feel the same. I think we should have our marriage annulled."

Gemma looked over at her husband and saw that his eyes had fallen closed again. Dratted man, he hadn't been listening to a word she'd said.

"Liam!" she shouted at him.

His eyes flew open and scoured her face. With a slow lazy he smile his gaze fell on hers with an intensity she didn't quite understand. He sat up and reached for her.

"Ah, lovely Gemma. Come here."

Seriously? Apparently alcohol consumption had turned her husband into an idiot. No way did she intend to get any closer to him.

"No. You're not listening to me. I don't think

that's a good idea." She scrambled backward and out of his reach.

"You're wrong, love. It's the best idea I've had in a long time."

Liam leaned forward, grabbed her hand and pulled her towards him. She fell forward and placed her hands on his shoulders to brace herself. He wrapped his arms around her and captured her lips with his. Heat filled her as he kissed her with an urgency she didn't understand. She opened her mouth in a gasp, and he took advantage by pushing his tongue inside. His tongue danced with hers and coaxed her into pressing deeper into his arms. She reached up and ran her hands through his light blond hair and pulled the strands firmly through her fingers.

He groaned and started to place light kisses on her cheeks and down her neck. He stopped to untie her wrapper and pushed it off her shoulders. She watched as it pooled at her feet. Liam slipped her nightgown over her shoulder so that her bosom gleamed brightly in the moonlight.

"Perfect." He caressed each breast with his hands and licked one of her tight nipples. A thousand sensations traveled down her body and merged into a bundle of energy between her thighs. Gemma's emotions were all over the place with each new feeling Liam brought out of her. He made her feel too much, but she wanted more from him than passion. She had to stop before it went too far. They needed to get the marriage annulled. If they consummated their marriage that option would no longer be available to them.

Gemma could feel him start to push her gown further down her body and trail kisses across her stomach as she stood before him. She held her breath and let herself get lost in his touch. For a brief moment, it was everything she wanted. She could pretend Liam loved her. Until reality snapped her back to the present—giving her a good look at what this would all mean. She couldn't give into her desire. As much as she'd like to be with Liam in every way possible it would only lead to a devastating heartbreak. She had to stop him... and soon, before it was too late. Everything he did to her had an amazing effect on her body, and she would kill to know how it all would feel, but the price was too high.

"Liam, we shouldn't be doing this," Gemma whispered.

He kept going as if deaf to the sounds around him. Completely engrossed in the task at hand, he ran the palm of his hand across her hips and with innate slowness trailed his fingers across her buttocks. As he explored, Gemma's body lit up into a tight, overwhelming tangle of need. He left a trail of heat with each caress. A long drawn out moan escaped her mouth as an unrelenting pressure built up inside her.

"That's right, love. Feel it, let go," Liam whispered in her ear. He continued to stroke her flesh as he spread kisses all over her neck and bosom.

She looked into her husband's eyes, and they reflected her own desire. They hadn't gone too far, yet. She could still stop this. But, she didn't want to. Liam made her feel so amazing. He played her body as adeptly as a violist plucked the strings of their instrument. Her body wanted him to keep going—to see where it all might lead. Gemma couldn't give into those base instincts. Her first instinct should be to protect her fragile heart. It thrummed so loud inside her chest it almost deafened her, as if it pleaded with her for mercy. This couldn't happen... she had to end it. Stepping back she pulled her gown back up and picked her wrapper up. Putting it back on, she tied it tightly across her breasts.

"What are you doing, Gemma?"

"This isn't why I came here, Liam. I don't want this."

"You could have fooled me, love. You were just moaning with pleasure."

"Pleasure is an empty feeling when there is no love to sustain it. I don't want this with you. I tried to tell you that, but you got lost in *your* wants," Gemma said with a wobbly voice.

"You're saying you don't want me."

She could hear the anger in Liam's tone. Rage laced with confusion and pain. She hadn't handled this well, but she had to protect her heart. Only he had the power to destroy her emotionally.

"Want is a relative term. I'm sure you could make me want you a whole lot. You demonstrated that rather well a few moments ago. I'm asking you to leave me be. I can't be intimate with someone when love is absent. I'd rather we didn't visit that aspect of our marriage."

"It's a mistake," Liam said.

"I don't believe so. I think it's the only way I can ensure neither one of us does something we will regret."

"It's already too late for that. Just go, Gemma. I'm still a little drunk, and I'm afraid I'll say something that will come back to haunt me later." Liam sat on the bed with his head bowed. He scrubbed his face with his hands.

"We should discuss..."

"I told you to leave. Please don't make me repeat myself, unless you're willing to stay and finish what we've already started." Derision filled his voice. "You've left me in quite a state of unrest. I might be willing to allow you to pleasure me in another way if you're so eager to stay."

Gemma could see a large bulge filling his breeches. It appeared to grow under her direct scrutiny. One day her curiosity would be her undoing, but today would not be that day. She would not allow herself to explore any part of Liam's gorgeous body.

"No need to be crude. I told you I hadn't come in here for that. It's not my fault you assumed I had."

"And yet you didn't mind it all that much when I touched you, did you?" He raised his eyebrows in question.

"Well, I can't deny it had a certain pleasantness to it. It doesn't mean I wish to repeat it. I will take your leave now."

She turned to go with as much dignity as she could muster. The sight of his growing manhood caused tingles to crawl up the base of her spine as nerves pooled in her belly. Part of her itched to reach out and touch him, to learn everything she could, but she couldn't give into that desire. She still had a deep-rooted need inside her. One she knew that only he could sate, and yet she also realized it could never happen. Not for the sake of her sanity.

"You can run, Gemma, but you can't hide. This thing between us can't be ignored." Liam laughed.

Gemma reached the door and turned to look at him. He still sat before her with his trousers now open and leaning his arms back against the bed. His gaze held every temptation she tried to escape from. Liam had always been her undoing. Too bad he also couldn't prove to be her salvation.

"Who said anything about hiding? I don't plan on going anywhere. Good night."

Gemma's heart raced and pounded against her chest. Things hadn't gone at all how she thought it would. Nothing ever did where Liam was concerned. He drove her mad, and she couldn't help how he made her feel. She had always loved him and no matter what,she knew she always would.

Her love had never been in question.

Gemma's position had already been laid out and stomped on. His feelings toward her were the reason she held back. She didn't lie to him. She needed more than pleasure, no matter how wonderful it made her feel. What she desired above anything else in the world was for her husband to love her. If she could make that a reality then her marriage would no longer be a sham. Nothing else could make her life any more perfect.

CHAPTER SEVEN

A constant drum of pain beat with a steady and consistent rhythm against Liam's skull. The afternoon sun streamed through the window, and he could feel its blinding intensity skimming across his eyelids. The very idea of opening his eyes made him want to turn over and cover his head with his pillow. Liam might consider it except a cold draft had settled over his body, and he struggled to get warm.

Why had he gone to bed without covering himself with a blanket?

Lifting one eyelid into a small slit to canvass the situation, it all came crashing back to him at the sight of his tousled bed. Gemma had come to see him, in his bedroom, and he'd made a fool of himself.

For one glorious moment, the experience held every fantasy that played through his mind. The pure bliss of holding her, tasting her, and hearing her soft moans filled him with an unsurpassable desire— until it all crashed and burned.

Liam remembered Noah had helped him up to his room and torn the bedsheets down his bed before finally pushing him onto it in a disorderly manner. Then, he had closed his eyes, oblivious to the world around him. That was until Gemma wandered into his room. Somehow his boots had been removed, but the particulars escaped his brain. The rest of his clothing, although messy and wrinkled, remained on his body as he lay on the bed. No doubt he should at least thank his friend for getting him this far; he'd probably have passed out at his club if not for his assistance.

His actions with his wife had been deplorable. He should apologize. Liam had decided not to explore that side of their marriage until they knew each other better. He'd blundered rather badly at the sight of her in her night clothes. When he opened his eyes and got a good look at her her need shot straight through him. All reason left him. Liam wanted her and he bloody hell wouldn't deny himself.

Perhaps she'd be in a forgiving mood. She'd come

into his room after all—not the other way around. He would talk to her and assess the situation. Maybe he still had a chance to win her over; to make her see that being with him was the best possible option for her.

With slow and deliberate movements, Liam pulled himself into a sitting position on the bed. Every muscle in his body ached, and his eyes were dry and gritty. He rubbed his face in an attempt to remove all the remnants of sleep from his mind and body. It didn't do much to help. He needed a bath and a shave. He reached up and pulled the bell to alert his valet he needed help. He didn't move an inch while he waited for Grady to arrive.

"You need assistance, sir?"

"Yes, Grady, I feel bloody awful. Please get a bath prepared."

"Very good, sir. I will see to it immediately. Would you like a tray brought up? You missed breakfast."

"Is it really afternoon? I was hoping that the sun was just especially bright and high this morning."

"Luncheon is in an hour, sir. It's now very late morning."

"No tray then. I will eat in an hour. Maybe by then I can tolerate food." His stomach rolled at the idea of eating. How much did he drink last night? "Where is my wife?"

"Lady Marsden is in the sitting room having tea. His Grace, the Duke of Huntly just arrived. She is entertaining him."

"Is she now? Skip the bath, Grady, help me shave and get dressed. I will probably have to go intervene. Noah made a mess of things with her yesterday."

Grady nodded and started to prepare everything to aid Liam. It didn't take long to get him ready to go downstairs. Less than twenty minutes later he was dressed, shaved, and at least on the outside, ready to face the world. The nauseous feeling still sat like a heavy brick inside him, but his outward appearance gave him a sense of confidence. The only thing left for him to do was go face his wife and best friend. He hoped he could make it through the whole meeting without falling over.

Liam strolled down the stairs and walked down the hallway to the sitting room. He could hear Gemma's melodious laughter resonate through the room. He stopped outside the doorway and leaned against the wall. The room began to spin, and he needed to get his bearings before he ambled his way into the room. While he stood there, he listened to their conversation.

"I assure you, Your Grace, you have nothing to apologize for," Gemma explained.

"I disagree, but let's just say we are at an impasse and move on. As long as you don't hold it against me."

"I don't see any reason I would. You were just looking out for your friend. I can't fault you for that. I kind of like that you were willing to go to such lengthy measures. It shows how loyal you are." Gemma grinned. "Although in hindsight it may have been amusing to see how far you would have taken it. You don't strike me as someone who would betray his best friend. If I had been in my right mind, I'd have tested you myself."

"I don't think I'd have survived. I'm glad you didn't have it in you to use your wiles against me. You would have wounded me forever."

"You may be right. It's best it played out as it did." Her laughter floated through the room.

Was Gemma flirting with Noah? No, he had to be imagining things again. She wouldn't do that, would she? It saddened him to admit that he didn't know her anymore. If last night was any indication, she no longer wanted him, but perhaps his friend held an appeal to her now. No way would he ever allow it. For a brief moment, Liam was blinded as he saw red flashing behind his eyes. An unknown emotion took root. One he'd never experienced before and had trouble identifying. His pulse raced and his hand shook. Liam clenched his fist at his side and closed his eyes. He took two deep calming breaths and imagined his wife with Noah—and heat fused through his whole body, again. Gemma's amusement brought him back to reality. He needed to get in that room; had to know where things stood with his wife.

He hobbled to the opening and got a glimpse of Gemma. She sat next to Noah on the settee, her hand resting in his. A sparkle shown in her eyes, bright red curls framed her face, and a happy smile beamed on her beautiful face. She looked radiant, and Noah appeared to be the reason.

"I'm not interrupting, am I?" With every ounce of energy he had in him, Liam sauntered into the room. He refused to show any weakness.

"I see you finally decided to crawl out of bed and join the rest of the world." Gemma frowned. "I almost wouldn't be able to guess you had gone out drinking last night. Of course, it probably helped to sleep off most of the nasty effects."

"So much concern for my health, ah… I see now the benefits of having a wife. You must care so much to harp on my actions so elegantly." Liam held his hand over his heart mocking her words. He strolled over and sat down on the chair next to the settee. "What, you didn't think to include me in your visit? No cup for me?"

"I didn't think to ask the servants to bring brandy with the tea, Liam. Forgive me for my oversight. I should correct it immediately." Scorn filled her voice.

"Good, see that you do. It's quite abysmal I don't have something to quench my thirst."

Gemma got up and walked out of the room stomping her feet each step of the way. The anger palpable on her face as her cheeks became as red as the curls framing it.

"Are you always so bloody asinine after drinking so much?" Noah asked raising his eyebrow at Liam. "Cause if so I don't recall you ever acting like an arse before now."

"Go bugger yourself, Noah. I'm not in the mood."

"Got up on the wrong side of the bed, did you?" Noah chuckled. "And here I thought you'd be glad to see me. I did make sure you made it home in one piece."

All of the laughter and amusement started to reverberate through his skull. It added a new layer of pain joining the already steady beat drumming inside his head.

"Not that I'm ungrateful, but I would prefer it if you didn't get too cozy with my wife." Liam scowled.

Noah sat back with shock on his face. "What the hell is that supposed to mean?"

"I heard you talking—flirting with Gemma. Leave her alone." Liam crossed his arms over his chest and stared at Noah with antagonism.

"I'm going to pretend that you are not accusing me of trying something with your wife. You know I wouldn't do that," Noah said baffled.

"Do I?" Liam raised an eyebrow. "You admitted to propositioning her last night."

"Damn it, Liam. Quit while you still can. You know last night wouldn't have happened. I do not want to become your wife's lover."

"Why the hell not?" Liam asked, insulted. "You don't think she's good enough for you?"

"I don't believe you! First you get on my case because you think I'm flirting with Gemma, and now you want to know why I'm not? What the bloody hell is going on in that head of yours?"

"Hell, if I know. Perhaps you should go before I say something else completely insane." Liam scrubbed his hands over his face in disgust. "This is what she is driving me to. I'll be in Bedlam before the day is out."

Gemma walked back in just as Noah stood up to leave.

"You're not leaving, are you? We were just getting to know each other," Gemma said.

Liam noticed Gemma's face light up as she looked at Noah. He had to repress the urge to get up and punch his best friend. Noah couldn't help that his wife liked him. Of course that didn't make him feel any better; the desire to pummel him didn't diminish as he watched her face glow brighter and happier in front of the duke.

"This is your doing, isn't it?" She turned to Liam, anger replacing the joy on her face. "I thought you were close? Why are you chasing him away?"

"He isn't making me leave, I assure you. I have business to take care of. I just wanted to apologize and make sure Liam had survived the night okay. It's time for me to take care of some other pressing matters."

"Oh, perhaps you can dine with us later in the week. I'd like to continue our discussion." Gemma smiled.

"Absolutely. Send a note as to what day and I will make sure I'm here," Noah said.

"Good. I look forward to seeing you again." Gemma grinned. "I'll send a note around later today."

Noah nodded at her and then turned back to Liam. "I will see you later. Perhaps you will be in a better mood."

"I doubt it," Liam grumbled.

"Good day, Lady Marsden," Noah said and left the room.

"What's wrong with you today?" Gemma demanded.

"Not a bloody thing. I'm just perfect. You, on the other hand, seem to like His Grace a little too much. It explains a lot actually."

"Are you still drunk?" She tilted her head to the side and scrunched her eyebrows up in confusion.

"Unfortunately no. Maybe I should be," Liam said. He stood up and walked over to her and stopped in front of her. "Or perhaps I still am, it would explain the lack of control I'm experiencing. Although I believe it's more apt to say you make me this way, dear."

"Don't blame me for your detestable behavior."

"I'm only giving credit where it's due, love."

"I'm not going to stand here and take this. I have better things to do with my time." Gemma started to leave, but Liam grabbed a hold of her hand and prevented her from storming out of the room.

"Like what? Chase after Noah?"

"I don't know where you are getting these delusional ideas from, but I am not interested in the Duke of Huntly."

"I don't believe you," Liam said as he pulled her into his arms. "But that's a matter for another day."

"Let me go."

"I can't. I will never let you go, Gemma."

He lowered his head and with a softness he didn't feel he pressed his lips to hers. She might want Noah now, but she had wanted him first. Liam just needed to remind her that she had loved him once and could again. It might take a while to get her to acknowledge it, but he had faith in his ability to duplicate that emotion within her. Gemma stood there and let him press light, innocent kisses on her lips and cheeks. Her actions made him believe she wasn't going to fight him... or encourage him.

"This isn't a good idea, Liam."

"Possibly not, but I needed to. I will leave you be for now, but Gemma you should be prepared."

"Whatever for?"

"A siege like you've never known before. I don't intend to give up easily. If you think you are going to turn to Noah you are mistaken. You are my wife, and I didn't take those vows lightly. I have never been good at sharing, and I'm not about to start this late in life."

"I told you I don't want the duke. Why can't you believe that? Never mind, I'm not going to argue with you. Believe what you want. I have better things to do."

With those words, Gemma stomped out of the room. Her face still held the red stains of anger on her cheeks or possibly a small amount could be attributed to his kiss. Liam hoped some of it could be accredited to her desire for him. That at least she couldn't fake or deny. The battle lines were clearly drawn and he intended to win the war. Gemma would belong to him in every way. In time, she would realize it too.

CHAPTER EIGHT

*G*emma stormed into the library and sat down on a chair and let out a muffled scream. That man infuriated her. How dare he accuse her of wanting the Duke of Huntly! Just because she entertained him while he visited did not mean a thing. She had no designs of being anything other than his friend. After they got past his faux pas, they had gotten along very well. As she spent more time with him, she found him quite charming and personable. For a brief moment, she was able to forget her troubles and just enjoy talking with someone else. The Duke of Huntly made it possible for her to laugh and smile for the first time since she had walked into her new home.

Liam, her husband, had only caused her

heartache. How had they come to be in such a place? He didn't want her, but he didn't want anyone else to have her either. He acted like a kid with a new toy. Playing with it when he wanted to and casting it aside after it no longer amused him. Although he hadn't had a chance to entertain himself with her; preventing that last night had taken all the strength she had within her. If Liam had once even pretended to love her, she would have acquiesced to his seduction.

Gemma got up and started to amble around the room. She stopped and looked at the various bookcases. Perhaps she should get a book to read... No, that didn't interest her. She had only retreated to the library to get away from Liam. Restlessness roamed through her, and she knew sitting still to read would prove to be impossible. Too much ran through her mind. She had to find a way to get Liam to agree to annul their marriage.

"Pardon me, but you have a visitor," Pemberly said.

GEMMA TURNED to look at the butler. He stood in the doorway awaiting her instructions. Who could be visiting her? The only friend she had in the world lived across the ocean in South Carolina.

"I'm not expecting anyone. Can you tell whoever it is I'm not in?"

"Now dear, I'm not one to be turned away."

Just behind the butler, Viscount Torrington filled the doorway. His dark hair tied at the nape of his neck; his blue eyes sparkled with mischief. He had a very large frame; Liam took after him in height and build. Lily adored her father and often said she took after him in temperament, but Gemma didn't know him all that well. She didn't want to start on that journey now. What she wanted was for them all to leave her be so she could think.

"Viscount Torrington, what can I help you with?" Gemma asked. She only barely kept her annoyance out of her voice. "Pemberly, can you have Janie bring in some refreshments?"

"No need, Pemberly. I won't be here long."

Gemma raised her eyebrow at him. "Maybe I'd like some."

"Do you?"

"No, but it's rude of you to presume I didn't." Gemma shot back at him.

"You've got spirit." He laughed. "I can see why Lily likes you."

"Well the feeling is mutual, I happen to adore your daughter," Gemma said. "I repeat, my lord, what can I help you with?"

"I came to see Liam, but Pemberly informed me I just missed him."

"He left?" Gemma asked surprised. Liam was so bloody rude. She clenched her fists at her side. "I hadn't realized."

Gemma strolled over to the chair she had vacated earlier and sat back down befuddled that he had already left. He didn't believe in letting her know anything. Just decided to leave and didn't care if she might want to know. That man could drive a saint crazy with his carelessness.

"Perhaps you can answer my questions. Liam was supposed to come by and see me last night. He failed to show up."

"What?" Confusion filled her voice. "I assumed he was leaving to go to his club—which he indeed did. He never mentioned going to see you last night."

"Liam went drinking?" Torrington raised his eyebrow. "That's entirely unlike him. What happened when he went to retrieve you yesterday?"

"Oh, that." Gemma snorted. "He lost his mind."

"How so?" the viscount inquired.

"When he got there, Alfie... let's say his hands

were roaming in places they didn't belong," Gemma explained. "Liam strolled in, took one look at us, and announced that he hoped my cousin wasn't doing what he thought to his *fiancée*."

"Well, that was part of the plan. He needed a reason to get you away from him. At least that worked well."

Stupid plan—of course, she must be too simple-minded to have been included in on the details of it. Nice to know the big broad gentlemen could take care of the helpless female. If only she could have inherited her funds sooner. Then she wouldn't have needed anyone's aide. Gemma would be in South Carolina with Lily.

"Yes, I gathered that much. I assume the contract was a scheme he concocted to help me leave without much fuss."

Maybe she could get some details out of Viscount Torrington. Liam hadn't been too forthcoming when she asked him questions. Gemma wasn't above getting information from another source.

"I don't know what you mean. The signatures on that contract are completely valid." Torrington smiled.

He was so smug. Gemma wanted to wipe the smile right off his face. She restrained herself from acting on it. Wouldn't be good to strike Viscount Torrington—he might not react well to it.

"Yes, I know. Both you and my father wanted to betroth us several years ago. I assume you didn't fully go through with it, or I'd have known about it. Regardless, it doesn't mean anything now. Your son used the contract to convince Alfie he and I were betrothed, and I left with him."

"Good, at least you don't have to worry about his less than desirable attentions. Anything else I need to know?"

"He also decided my cousin needed to be taught a lesson. I didn't get to witness that. He wouldn't allow it. After I left the room, he took care of it."

"So far I'm not hearing anything to indicate he is going crazy," Torrington said. "I'd have done the same."

"Yeah, I'm sure you don't." Gemma smiled. "But then you didn't get the joy of experiencing it all."

"Too true," Torrington said. "I'm glad he was able to help you. I hate that Lily worried over your safety. So when are you set to sail to South Carolina?"

"I don't know." Gemma shrugged her shoulders. "He did say we'd go there for our wedding trip. He's been... strange since we left the vicarage."

"Wait, the vicarage?" Torrington's eyes widened.

His mouth fell open for several seconds. He shook his head, disbelief clouding his eyes. "Are you saying you actually got married yesterday?"

Wait... they weren't supposed to get married? Did she just read him right? Why had Liam married her when that part wasn't included in the plan? A little flutter took root in her heart—hope. Dangerous, but she couldn't stop it from expanding into something full-fledged deep inside her.

"Well, yes. I thought that was the plan? Liam didn't exactly fill me in on all the details. Just said I had to go along with it, or I'd end up unhappily married to Alfie. Don't get me wrong, I am grateful I didn't have to travel down that road, but I didn't exactly want to trade one unhappy marriage for another."

Torrington rubbed his temples with his fingers. Gemma could relate to his frustrations. Liam had deviated from whatever plan they hitched together. She had to wonder what he had been supposed to do. After a few moments and several different plays of emotions crossing his face, he looked at Gemma with a humorous smile on his face.

"You're right." Torrington nodded in agreement.

"Of course I'm right." She pressed her lips

together and tilted her head to the side. "But please explain what you think I'm right about."

"That boy has lost his bloody mind." Torrington laughed.

Nice to see one of them found humor in this situation.

"I fail to see why that is so funny."

"You would, dear, you would. This is going to be quite entertaining." Torrington chuckled.

Gemma crossed her arms over her chest and stomped her foot.

"I'm glad that your son going insane amuses you so. I don't share in that sentiment as I have to live with him. Will you please quit laughing! It isn't that funny."

Heat filled Gemma's cheeks as she watched the hilarity take over her father-in-law. The viscount now laughed so hard he had trouble breathing. His face turned red and he held his stomach with his arms.

"I can't wait to tell Pia that her baby boy finally got himself hitched," he said after he gained some composure. "By and by, welcome to the family. I should get home and let my wife in on the good news."

"Hmph, tell her I said hello and to come visit

soon. Her company at least is something I can look forward to. The men in this family lack manners."

"We make up for it in other ways. Tell Liam I stopped by and to come see me soon."

Gemma watched as Liam's father left the library. She waited until she could no longer hear his footsteps in the hall and left to return to the sitting room. Her reason for hiding out in the library had left the townhouse. Liam would no doubt return at some point, but for now she had a little breathing room. What she couldn't understand was why his father had found the situation so hilarious. To her, nothing about being married to Liam was amusing. She still had to find a way to get out of it. Perhaps she should just arrange to travel to see Lily. As a married woman, she didn't have quite the same constraints as a young miss. Yes, that idea appealed to her, maybe marrying Liam wasn't an entirely bad thing. She'd look into the requirements and possibilities. Lily would be able to help her sort through the shambles of her life. Maybe she'd also have some insight on how to deal with her unruly brother.

CHAPTER NINE

*L*iam opened the front door to his parents townhouse and walked inside. He traveled down the hallway and stopped just outside his father's study. He had to update him on everything that happened.

He had no idea where to even begin to explain everything.

His father had been the last thing on his mind. Nothing had gone the way he had planned. No, what happened was the world had spiraled out of control, and he didn't have the first clue on how to get it all back on track.

Marrying Gemma was never part of the plan. That part was supposed to be a farce, but he lost his mind when he walked in and saw Alfie's hands all over her. Something snapped inside him, and all he could think about was breaking her cousin's neck.

Once he had her safely tucked away in his carriage his heart had calmed. It made it a little easier to think rationally. It was in those moments he realized the only way he could keep her safe was to marry her. In his mind that course of action made sense because he could ensure no one ever hurt her again.

Liam didn't take into consideration his growing desire. He wanted Gemma in ways he'd never imagined. She made his heart beat faster, and he itched to explore every inch of her. He wanted to see her smile—for him alone. A sultry one that bespoke of pleasure and passion, but also one that sparkled with inner happiness. Liam needed her to be all right with their marriage and to accept every aspect of it.

He should have taken her feelings into consideration—in some ways he was no better than Alfie. Liam had presumed to know what was best for her. The only difference was he'd at least respect her wishes. Liam would never force himself on her. Gemma clearly didn't want him any longer. He had wrongly assumed she would be ecstatic to be his wife.

It was equally apparent what a bloody fool he'd turned into.

"Liam, why are you just standing there?"

He turned to see his mother standing in the hallway. Her pale blond hair twisted into a chignon and her blue eyes filled with concern. Not once had he thought about how he would explain it all to her. She wanted her children to be happy. She would not be pleased to see him all tied up in knots over Gemma.

"Hello mother," Liam strolled over and gave her a quick hug. "I came to see Father. We have some things to discuss."

"Oh well, you missed him. He left a while ago." She studied him for a few moments and nodded . "You will join me for tea and tell me what's troubling you."

Liam gulped as he prepared himself for her interrogation. He wiped his hands on his pants to remove the moisture beading on his palms.

His mother could always see right through him. Escaping was completely out of the question. She didn't ask him to join him, but rather demanded it. Liam didn't want to disappoint her and dreaded the upcoming conversation.

He did the only thing he could in this situation.

Liam turned on his heels and followed her to her sitting room. Once inside, she gestured for him to take a seat in one of the chairs as she sat down on the settee.

"I already ordered tea when I heard you walk in the door. I haven't had a chance to visit with you in a while. I wanted to catch up. As soon as I saw you I knew something bothered you, and now you can tell me what is on your mind. Perhaps I can help."

How could he explain to his lovely mother that he had made a mess of his life and had no clue where to even begin straightening it out? She sat there with her hands folded in her lap, and her face turned towards him with questions radiating from her eyes.

"It's a long story."

"Lucky for you I have plenty of time."

"I don't know where to begin..."

"I'd say you start from where the issue began. Don't leave any details out. If I'm to help, I need to know everything."

Everything? No, he couldn't tell her it all. Not a chance in hell would he tell her about what happened between him and Gemma in his bedroom the night before. Some things one just didn't discuss with their mother.

"I guess it began with Lily's letter."

"I need more than that. Lily writes often. Which letter?"

"She wrote to Father about her concern for Gemma. Are you aware of her situation?" Liam asked.

"Yes. I know that her cousin is trying to force her to marry him."

"Not going to bloody happen—" Liam muttered under his breath. He clenched his fists tight against his legs.

"What was that Liam?"

Liam forced himself to relax and unclenched his fists. He had to be careful before he went off on a tangent. He needed to stick to the facts or he didn't have a chance of getting through this conversation.

"Alfie isn't going to marry Gemma," Liam said.

"Oh, that's good. I know Lily will be relieved. I'm confused though how you can say for sure that will not happen."

Liam sucked in a deep breath and slowly exhaled. Now he needed to tell her that he married the girl himself. He had no idea how she would react to the news. She liked Gemma, at least he believed she did.

"Uh, well, he can't marry her because she is already married to someone else."

"Really? How wonderful for her. When did she

get married and what is the lucky gentleman's name?"

Her face glowed with happiness that Gemma had found someone to share her life with. That was a good sign. She did want her to be happy, so he hoped she was also okay with her being his wife. He didn't want to add to Gemma's stress. He already fought an uphill battle where she was concerned.

"Liam, you're not answering me. Is it a bad thing that she is married to a different gentleman? Is this what is bothering you?"

"Yes and no."

"Yes, it's a bad thing or yes it's bothering you. Quit stalling and just tell me what is going on."

His mother's hands flew up in the air. Her lips pursed as her eyes narrowed into slits, studying him.

"No, it's not a bad thing. At least I don't think so. I married her yesterday by special license." Liam got up and paced. He stopped a few feet away and turned back to her. "Yes, it is what is bothering me. I've made a bit of a mess of things with her."

A whoosh of relief flooded him. He returned to his seat and relaxed back into it. There he finally got it all out. Now he just had to sit back and pray his mother reacted well to the news. She was a bit unpredictable at times. He never knew what to expect with her.

"Oh," she said in a quiet tone. She sat back and folded her hands in her lap. Her gaze drifted to the wall behind him. She tilted her head and studied some innocuous object. Her mouth hung open for several seconds and then softened into a half smile, but she didn't say another word.

That's it? All she had to say was oh? That didn't leave him with anything to go by. She said she would help him, and she didn't have anything to say about the situation?

"What? You don't have any other reaction? I expected more than that out of you," Liam said.

"I've never been at a loss for words before. I didn't expect you to say you married her. Yes, I knew how she felt about you, but I also thought you were nowhere near ready to settle down with anyone. You vehemently stated that on more than one occasion. I guess I am a bit shocked and confused."

"You and me both. I can't explain it. I don't quite know how it all happened. It wasn't the plan, and yet it feels so right."

"Tell me how this all came about. I know Lily had concerns, and your father had an idea about how to extricate Gemma from the situation. He didn't explain it to me, and I didn't think to ask."

"The original plan was to get Gemma on a ship and take her to live with Lily in South Carolina. Father did ask me if I had feelings for her first. He didn't want to ship her off if I wanted her for myself. He suggested I marry her if I wanted her. It was a good solution to save her." Liam paused and took a moment to catch his breath. "At the time I said no. I had no intention of tying our lives together. I didn't want her hurt though, so I agreed to help Gemma and make sure she arrived safely in Lily's care."

"So how did you end up getting married? If you didn't want to be with her why put yourself through so much unnecessary pain. You both deserve better than that."

"I hope it won't all be pain. I want a happy life with, Gemma, but I messed up. I tossed her aside when she expressed her feelings to me two years ago. I was cavalier with her and laughed. I was too young and didn't know what I would ultimately be giving up."

"You love her," his mother said in a soft tone.

Did he? Noah had suggested it, but he had tossed it aside as nonsense. He cared for her. But love? That was an entirely different thing. Liam pictured

Gemma. Her gloriously vibrant red hair and her alluring green eyes—he definitely desired her.

"How does one know when they are in love?"

His mother paused and studied him. "That's not an easy question to answer."

"Then how will I know if I love her?"

"Let me ask you this," she tilted her head. "How do you feel when you are not with her?"

The question didn't make any sense to him. What did being away from Gemma have to do with being in love with her? His mother wasn't helping at all. This was just leading to more confusion.

"What do you mean?"

"You're here with me. How do you feel about leaving Gemma alone?" A knowing glint took root in her eyes. "How would you feel if she insisted on going to live with Lily in South Carolina?"

Not bloody happening. Gemma was never leaving him. He clenched his fists again, and his breathing became more ragged. Liam could feel heat filling his cheeks and spreading down his neck.

"Gemma belongs with me."

"Do you feel that way because you see her as one of your possessions?" Her tone was the mask of innocence. She had no expression on her face.

"Of course not," Liam's mouth hung open as he

sputtered for words. "Gemma isn't an object. She deserves to be happy.

"She certainly does, but what if that's not with you?"

Liam sat back and considered her words. She had a point. What if Gemma couldn't be happy with him? No, he wouldn't consider that as a possibility. He loved her—Oh God. His heart sped up and beat hard inside his chest. He did love her. Liam could make her happy. He'd just have to find a way to make her see she belonged with him.

"Let me ask you one more question. It might help you to understand your motivations." His mother leaned forward and looked him in the eyes. "If you didn't know you loved her why did you marry her?"

"It was pure instinct. I walked in and saw Alfie with his hands all over her, and I saw red. I reacted and just went with it. It felt right so it had to be the best decision." He paused and scrubbed his hands over his face. This was such a mess. "The problem now is she no longer feels the same way. She doesn't want me, and I'm not much better than Alfie. I forced her to marry me because I thought it was best for her. I refuse to give up though."

"Then you shouldn't."

"I don't know where to even begin..."

"I think you've always had deep feelings for her. You got them all clouded up in that stupid betrothal agreement. Let it all go and just tell her how much you want to be with her."

"You think it's that easy? Just tell her I love her and hope it reminds her she loves me too? I don't think it will work that way." Liam got up and paced again. "What did I do before to make her love me? I need to do that again if I can only figure out what it was."

A laugh rolled through the room and bounced off the walls echoing around him. He looked at his mother and realized the sound came from her. She found his troubles amusing? There was something strangely perverse about her finding his issues entertaining.

"I fail to see why this is so funny," he said.

"Darling you didn't *do* anything to make her fall in love with you. It just is what it is. I doubt she fell out of love with you to begin with. She loved who you are or who she believed you were. Just be yourself and tell her how you feel. Gemma just needs to know you feel the same way. She isn't going to lay her heart on the line again and have it stomped on. You hurt her and she is just protecting herself. It's up to you to make the next move. She isn't going to do it for you."

Was his mother right? Is it really that simple? *Does Gemma still love me?* He had to find out and try it. Maybe he just needed to let her know that she meant the world to him.

"You believe that? I just can't believe it's that easy."

"Life is only as hard as you make it. If you want to make things work in your marriage, you need to open up and talk to your wife. Nothing gets solved by closing yourself off and ignoring the problem. Maybe I'm wrong, but I doubt it."

"All right. I will talk with Gemma. I should be honest with her. It took me long enough to realize I love her. It's only right I am as sincere with her as she was with me in the past. I only hope it's enough."

"It's all you can do. Let me know how things go. Did you still need to talk to your father? I don't know when he will return."

He didn't want to repeat this conversation with his father. The viscount would probably goad him a lot more than his mother did with her laughter. He had an even more wicked attitude than she had. Probably a leftover remnant from his pirating days...

"Could you fill him in on the details? If he still

needs to talk to me have him send word and I will return another day."

"I can do that. I can handle your father. I think we need to have a little talk ourselves."

Amusement filled him—it might be interesting to stick around and see their chat. His mother tended to break things when she was mad at his father. If he wasn't mistaken, she seemed a little irritated when she said they needed to talk. He had better things to do though. Gemma was his only concern for the moment.

Liam nodded . "Thank you, mama. I didn't realize how much I needed to talk about this."

"Anytime. Go and talk to Gemma. Straighten out your marriage."

Liam turned and walked out of the room. A new sense of purpose blossomed inside him. He had a lot to do, and he knew just where he would start with Gemma. He should have seen it himself. Why would she open up to him if she still believed he didn't return her feelings? His mother was right. He would plan something special and tell her everything.

CHAPTER TEN

The viscount's departure left Gemma with a mix of emotions. Her stomach churned within her. She held her hand over her midsection in an attempt to calm the queasiness setting in. This marriage business didn't sit well with her. She had a father-in-law struck by the hilarity of it and a husband who didn't stick around long enough to be one. Gemma desperately needed something to keep her mind off the last days tumultuous events. The best course of action was to get engrossed in an activity that was both time-consuming and mentally draining. Which gave her an idea... wouldn't it be wonderful to attend a function later that evening? It would give her a reason to be absent and something to keep her mind busy. Maybe if she weren't home, she wouldn't be so painfully aware of her husband's lack of attention.

If she was going to go out, she needed to know what social events were taking place. She remembered Janie had informed her of a stack of neglected invitations. Going through each one would give her something to occupy herself with until later. Gemma sat down at the writing desk in the library to look at those that had arrived over the past week. From the amount of unopened invitations, it seemed rather obvious her husband loathed socializing.

Gemma had taken a liking to attending events when she became friends with Lily. Prior to that fated meeting she had garnered similar feelings towards interacting with the ton that Liam seemed to have. The ton writhed with gossipmongers and pariahs, but it had also just as many wonderful individuals encased within it. She had learn that lesson the hard way. After her father's sudden death, she had to withdraw from society a bit as the rules of mourning hadn't allowed her to go to many balls or soirees.

Gemma didn't see any reason not to attend a few social events. She didn't need Liam to escort her and had no problem going on her own. There were still a few people that she could socialize with since most of her new friends were married themselves.

She picked up the first invitation. Ironically it was from Lady Silverton. Lily had met her husband, Rand, at the Silverton Ball three years prior. Gemma believed it a fitting occasion to instill her newfound freedom as a matron, instead of a maid. She may not feel married, but that didn't mean she couldn't take advantage of it. The more she thought about it, the more she realized marrying Liam might be the best thing that happened to her. Yes, he was a complete idiot, but she could work with that. She intended to enjoy a few social events and then make plans to visit Lily in South Carolina.

Gemma placed the invitation to the Silverton Ball in the accept pile. The ball was for later that evening, but that didn't matter. It was well-known Lady Silverton expected everyone to be present at her ball and prepared for those that decided to attend at the last minute. After going through each invitation, she decided on three that she would like to attend. Besides the ball she had a garden party and a musical she decided to attend.

She also had her dinner party to plan. With that in mind, she drafted invitations for her own party to Liam's parents, the Viscount and Viscountess

Torrington, the Duke of Huntly, and her friend Pearla Montgomery. After Lily had left for South Carolina, she became good friends with Pearla. If not for their friendship she may have become a wall-flower once again. In a lot of ways, Pearla reminded her of Lily. She had a dislike of marriage that rivaled Lily's. Lily caved when she met Randall Collins and gave marriage another look because of him. Perhaps Pearla would do the same one day.

"Ma'am, Cook said to let you know dinner will be ready in an hour. Is there any correspondence you need me to post?"

Gemma looked up at the butler as she sealed the last invitation to be delivered.

"Yes, Pemberly. I have three invitations for a dinner party in two nights. Can you make sure they are delivered? Also have Janie come in. I would like to discuss plans for the dinner party with her before we sit down to our meal tonight.

"Very well, ma'am. I shall send her in. If you give me the invitations, I will have a footman deliver them personally."

"Thank you Pemberly." Gemma handed all of the letters to him. "I also have two acceptances to post as well." As for the invitation to the Silverton Ball, she would accept in person later that evening. Thankfully all of her trunks had arrived earlier in the day. Otherwise, she would have had to decline for lack of a ball gown to wear.

Pemberly took all of her notes and left the room. Gemma straightened up the writing desk and pulled out a clean sheet of stationary. She dipped her quill in an ink pot and began making a list for the dinner party. A short time afterward Janie entered.

"Lady Marsden, Pemberly said you required my assistance."

"Yes, Janie. I am having a dinner party in two nights. I have made a list of what I would like for the meal and everything I require. Can you please make sure that all of this is completed?"

"Yes, ma'am." Janie took the list and examined it.

"Do you have any questions?"

"No. This is pretty clear. I will let Cook know what you would like for the meal. If she has any questions I will let you know after I speak with her," Janie said.

"Very well. I shall retire to the sitting room until dinner is served. "

Janie nodded and left the room. Gemma got up and went to the sitting room. As soon as she sat down, Liam walked into the room.

"Ah, there you are."

"I haven't exactly been hiding." Gemma's sarcasm evident in each word she spoke.

"I never said you were. I just couldn't locate you when I first arrived home."

"I was in the library going through invitations. I accepted a couple and wrote out a few for the dinner party I plan on having in a couple of days. You should know I invited your parents, the Duke of Huntly, and my friend Pearla. I hope you will deign to attend, so I have even numbers."

"Of course I will be here. I'd never be so rude."

"Right." Gemma rolled her eyes. Liam rude? Never. That's why he was making sure she was comfortable in her new home and paying a lot of attention to her. "Anyway everything is planned. All you need to do is show up."

"You said you accepted a couple of invitations for social events. Which one did you accept?"

Gemma didn't see any reason not to inform him of her plans. Maybe if he knew what they were, he would leave her be.

"A musical at the Carrington's and a garden party the Duchess of Westland is hosting. I also plan on attending Lady Silverton's ball tonight. Don't worry I can attend on my own. You have no need to come."

She wasn't sure if she wanted him to attend or

not. A small part of her hoped he would while the part of her irritated with him just wanted Liam to leave her in peace. What would be the point of escaping to a ball if he were fast on her heels? It was best to dispense with the notion of him attending at once. Gemma didn't want him to feel obligated after all.

"Ridiculous. I can escort my wife to a ball. I will be ready when you are."

Gemma sighed. He couldn't possibly want to attend the ball with her. From what she recalled he hated escorting Lily. She'd rather he just let her go alone. It would give her the opportunity to spend some time with her friends and enjoy herself. She didn't want to worry about the gossip mills or Liam's belligerence. He'd no doubt have an attitude all evening.

"It isn't necessary. I'd prefer to go alone. Do whatever you had planned for the evening. I am perfectly capable of going on my own."

Gemma fidgeted in her seat. Her lips pursed in displeasure as she looked up at him. How to get him to change his mind? It would be damned annoying to have him around all night. If he attended, no doubt he would ruin the whole evening brooding over everything she did. He had reacted badly just by her being nice to his best friend earlier that day. All she did was be polite to him and attempt to get to know him better. The Duke of Huntly appeared to be a charming and caring man.

"I have no other plans this evening. I had hoped to spend it with you. We have a lot we need to discuss."

"As far as I'm concerned we have talked more than I care. Keeping the peace works best if you don't open your mouth too much. I might start to like you a little better if you were mute more often."

Liam opened his mouth to speak and closed it in a tight firm line. His displeasure evident on his face as his eyes narrowed, and his brows bunched together while his forehead crinkled.

It was almost adorable—no, it definitely was. How cute. He wasn't happy. Too bad for him. Gemma hadn't been in the best of moods herself. She couldn't help admiring how absolutely gorgeous he was though. It made it difficult at times to stay mad at him. Why couldn't things have gone differently? All she wanted to do was wrap her arms around him and erase his discontent. She sighed. If his feelings mirrored hers she might just do it. She knew better though.

"Is it necessary to be so rude?" Liam asked.

Yes, it was—it made a fine defense mechanism. She needed as many as she could muster to keep her wits about her. Liam had the ability to leave her brainless, if she allowed it.

"I am only speaking my mind."

Gemma stood up and walked over to the window and looked out at the busy London street. She didn't want to argue with her husband, but she had to put a wall up between them. If she opened herself up to him again, it would lead to her downfall. The more time she spent with him the more it added to her chances of falling for him all over again. Gemma refused to love him any more than she already did.

"I am not allowing you to go to the ball on your own. If you want to attend, then expect me to be your escort."

Gemma turned to him and pinned him with her gaze. He was being mulish on purpose. He couldn't possibly want to attend. Why was he so determined to ruin everything for her? Heat filled her cheeks and spread throughout her body. She clenched the folds of her skirts in her hands. She gritted her teeth and took a few deep breaths.

"If that is the only way I can go, then I will plan on you accompanying me. I don't see why you are being so difficult."

"It's my prerogative. If you will excuse me, I have a few things to take care of before dinner is served."

Liam damn near stomped out of the room. His cheeks were flushed red with his anger. Gemma didn't see any reason why he'd be so upset. She gave him plenty of opportunities to stay home. She certainly wasn't forcing him to go to the ball. She turned on her heels to go sit back down. Her whole body shook after the confrontation. Damn him for unnerving her. Her hand trembled as she brushed it over her hair to smooth it in place. She needed some distance from Liam if she wanted her heart to remain unscathed.

It might prove futile because her heart and mind already headed towards a collision of uncertainty.

One wanted desperately to love him and believe he could love her; the other only wanted to protect the already bruised emotions housed deep inside its depths. At some point, the conflict must be resolved, or an implosion would occur. Gemma didn't know how much longer she could hold off all of her unresolved feelings.

In that moment, she decided to step up her plans to visit Lily. The plan no longer a want, it now upgraded to an urgent necessity to ensure her continued existence. If she stayed in England, she would lose a part of herself and she wanted to hold on to every piece of who she'd grown into over the past three years. Her independence and ability to stand up for herself depended on proving a point to Liam.

The man expected her to bow down to his every command. He had a hard lesson to learn, and Gemma knew how to teach it to him. With a plan hatching in her mind, Gemma smiled for the first time since her husband barged into the sitting room. Liam didn't have a clue what she truly could make happen. He would discover the truth soon enough. She only hoped it would happen before her heart and mind collided.

CHAPTER ELEVEN

*L*iam stomped up the stairs to his room to change for the ball his wife insisted on attending that evening. Gemma had excused herself an hour ago to prepare for the festivities. Liam decided he needed some liquid courage to get through the evening and instead of immediately getting ready for the ball, he went to his study and poured himself a snifter of brandy. He gulped down the first glass and nursed the second one for almost an hour.

Nothing went as he had planned.

When he left his parents' home, his intentions had been to tell Gemma exactly how much he loved and adored her. But, she turned on him as soon as she laid eyes on him. Her scathing retorts had put him on the defensive. Instead of a meaningful conversation they'd had a stilted one. It wasn't even a heated argument. He stood in front of her like a fool issuing proclamations.

She was driving him mad.

How could he possibly tell her what was inside his heart if she didn't even allowed him a chance to speak? So in lieu of a wonderful evening filled with love he was following her to the Silverton Ball. Every step of the way Gemma fought him, and his purpose was constantly thwarted.

Dinner that evening had been a silent affair. She didn't say one word to him through the entire meal. She said very little to the staff serving them. If Liam were to hazard a guess, she pretended he didn't exist while she ate. His state of nerves amounted to a bundle of repressed energy. At any moment, they would explode and leave a wake of devastation in their path. If he didn't gain control of the situation, he would not be held responsible for his actions. They had only been married a couple of days, and he was already ready to collapse from the sheer torture. He knew that not all ton marriages were love matches, far from it, in fact. Marriage in his family was different though.

They married for love even if it didn't appear to

be on the outside looking in. The world thought his parents' married because his father had forced his mother to in his pirating days. On a small scale, they were right. He did force her, but not entirely for the revenge everyone believed. He married her because he loved her and couldn't imagine a world without her by his side. That was how Liam saw his marriage to Gemma.

When he looked at her, he saw exactly how their life could be if only she would allow them a fraction of happiness. Instead, she fought him every step of the way. Liam didn't blame her entirely. This path had been created two years prior when he foolishly pushed Gemma away. It was his mistake, and he needed to rectify it. If he couldn't fix things, his life would fracture and he would never again be whole.

He wasn't about to give up on them. She would listen to him. Tonight he would make her hear the words he'd found it difficult to assimilate. Liam loved Gemma. It had just taken him longer to see what was right in front of him. Gemma was *his*. She'd always been the one woman meant for him. It was time to stop being nice and stake his claim in every way possible.

Liam finished dressing without the aid of his valet. With the state of his current mood, he thought it best to not inflict it on anyone else unnecessarily. After he tied his cravat, he walked out of his room and strolled back down the stairs. Gemma hadn't yet emerged from her bedroom, so he found himself fidgeting at the bottom of the stairs awaiting her arrival. He didn't have a whole lot of patience for anything.

Finally, he caught sight of her at the top of the stairs. She was a vision. Her emerald green ball gown fit her curves and cascaded down her hips to her ankles. The bodice was draped in lace and silk organza. Tiny green beads wrapped around her waist in an intricate pattern depicting a belt of flowers that trailed down the side of her overlaying skirt. Gemma's crimson hair were twisted around her head and plaited into a long braid that coiled at the nape of her neck. Tiny ringlets were curled framing her face with a small emerald hair adornment twinkling on the left side of her head.

Watching her descend the stairs Liam was breathless with anticipation. He wanted nothing more than to pull her into his arms and kiss her. The only thing that would be better was to turn her back around and march her upstairs to his room. Once there, he could slowly undress her as he savored every inch of her delectable body.

Why couldn't he kiss her? He should—it would be a start in the direction he hoped to head.

"I hope you haven't been waiting long. I had quite a bit to do to prepare myself for the ball."

Liam stepped toward her and caressed her cheek with the tips of his fingers. Her gaze locked with his. Her breathing became ragged as she gulped in air in short fast bursts.

"What are you doing?"

Liam didn't answer her with words. He leaned down and placed a soft kiss on her lips. Her mouth opened up as she gasped. It gave him an advantage, and he saw no reason not to take it. The tip of his tongue touched hers as he pulled her tighter in is embrace. Liam coaxed her with his mouth—wanting to fill her with every inch of desire coursing through his veins. She needed to be with him every step of the way. This was only the beginning of his fight to own every inch of her soul. Her body relaxed against him, and he took it as a sign. She wasn't as immune to him as she wanted him to believe. Gemma still wanted him. He could use that and he would.

Liam took a step back, pleased with what he saw. Gemma's eyelids were closed, her lips slightly parted and moist, and her cheeks a pretty pink. Her eyelashes fluttered up, and irises of green fire met his—she looked both a little dazed and well pleasured. They could move forward now. He'd managed to get her exactly where he wanted her.

"The carriage awaits us outside. I think it is time for us to depart."

Gemma looked a little dazed, but in a good way. She looked well pleasured. A confident arrogance took root deep inside her. He'd done that—built a craving in her she'd never experienced before. Soon he'd make sure she got a taste of it all.

Gemma cleared her throat and shook her head. She looked up at him and nodded. "Very well."

Liam hooked her arm over his and for the first time that evening believed that they may have a chance. She hadn't once snapped at him since she walked down the stairs.

"You look lovely; by the way. I love the color green on you."

"I didn't dress to please you, Liam. This just happens to be one of my new favorite ball gowns. I haven't had a chance to wear it yet, and this seemed like the perfect time to do so."

Maybe she hadn't—somehow he doubted it though. His lips tilted into a half smile as his gaze traveled over her.

"Doesn't make you any less beautiful to me. I quite enjoy how it looks on you."

Gemma didn't respond to his compliment—just stared at him in silence. He meant every one of his words. The dress enhanced her beauty and made her even more exquisite. Maybe going to this ball wasn't an entirely bad idea. Dancing would give him the chance to hold her in his arms and stare into the depths of her light green eyes. Perhaps it would remind her of the times they danced previously. He needed all the help he could get to help her realize she still loved him.

They exited the townhouse and walked over to the awaiting carriage. Liam helped Gemma inside and hopped in after she took her seat. Once the door closed, the driver nudged the horses into moving and they were on their way to the ball.

"I haven't been to a ball in quite a while. I don't socialize unless I am required to do so," Liam said.

Gemma's gaze was off to the side as she looked out the window of the carriage. She was doing her best to ignore him. Liam didn't want her to forget the heat between them. He needed to draw her back into his circle of warmth.

"I remember you always hated escorting Lily to

all of her social events," she said, still looking outside.

"When did you start attending social occasions again?"

A distance was starting to form again. Liam didn't like it one bit.

She turned to look at him. "You mean after my father died? I just began ordering ball gowns and more appropriate clothing a few months ago. I haven't been out much. Alfie didn't allow it. I had a seamstress visit me at home to prepare the gowns before he could prevent it from happening. Otherwise, I wouldn't have any new gowns at all. He even sequestered me. I couldn't visit my friends or having them visit with me. Although the only person that tried, besides the day you came to retrieve me, was Pearla. No one else realized anything was wrong. I managed to get someone to mail a few letters to Lily, but a lot of my missives got confiscated by my nefarious cousin. I despaired of ever being allowed outside the walls of my former home ever again."

"I hadn't realized that the situation had gotten so dire. At least Lily was able to contact my father."

"Hmmm yes. Speaking of your father, he stopped by while you were out. We had an interesting discussion."

"Really?" Liam raised his eyebrows.

What had his father done? Did he make the situation worse with Gemma? No, that wasn't possible. He messed up all on his own. Still, he'd plan on having a conversation with him to get all of the details of his visit.

"He was under the impression the plan hadn't included us getting married. He agreed with me that you are losing your mind."

"I assure you my mind has all of its faculties intact."

"We will have to agree to disagree. I just haven't seen much evidence to the contrary."

"I admit my behavior... has been less than savory lately. In my defense, you do drive me to the point of insanity at times."

Gemma looked him directly in the eyes. She pursed her lips as anger filled her eyes. Sparks flew out of them as her brows drew closer together, and her forehead crinkled in displeasure.

"You dare blame me for your turbulent moods? I have no control over your emotional state. Don't pretend I do for even a moment. I won't have you hold me responsible for your bad attitude."

That's much better. He enjoyed having her all to himself. All of her emotions steamrolling forward, right in his general direction. Liam tilted his head back and studied her. A half smile filled with cockiness spread across his face.

"Aren't you? I am usually an even-tempered person. Since I married you, I have been one big mess of disturbing outbursts. I can't seem to control what my next action may or may not be. I think you are entirely at fault for my state of being since I first walked in and saw Alfie attacking you."

"I'm not going to argue with you. You are clearly out of your mind. I intend to have fun tonight, and I refuse to allow you to ruin my good mood."

Good mood? Liam restrained from laughing. Who did she think she was fooling? She was most definitely *not* in a good mood.

"Fine. I only have one request."

"And what makes you think I will honor it?"

"Because if you don't I will instruct the driver to turn the carriage around and take us home."

"Oh, all right, you win. What do you want?"

"I want you to put me down for the first waltz of the evening."

Gemma crossed her arms across her chest and glared at him.

"No. I don't want to dance with you."

Liam sighed. Gemma would argue with him

about anything. If he said the sun rose in the sky she'd shake her head and tell him that it did not raise, it, in fact, fell each day. Why couldn't she agree to one dance? What made her want to avoid him? The kiss they'd shared seemed to sear right through her. Was she afraid of her feelings? It was time to test her reserve.

"Very well. I shall inform the driver we wish to skip the ball."

"No. I will put you on my dance card. You don't have to be so difficult. I don't even know why we are arguing about this. Never once did you want to dance with me willingly in the past. Lily had to practically force you too."

"Times change, I'm not the same man I was a couple years ago." Liam looked her in the eyes, pleading her to give in, accept him once more. He reached for her hand and rubbed his thumb over her palm. "Just give me a chance to prove it to you."

The green depths of her eyes remained unmoving. She studied him for several seconds. He kept moving the pad of his thumb over her hand, coaxing her into compliance. Her expression softened, her lips parted, and the tension left her body.

"I don't know if I'm willing to take that risk. A dance is more than I want to give to you, but I will acquiesce to your demands. I want to attend the ball, and I'm willing to do whatever is necessary to make that happen."

"I will take whatever you are willing to give me. In time I hope it's everything. For now I will settle for a dance."

Gemma didn't say anything else for the rest of the journey to the Silverton Ball. Liam allowed her to remain silent. He said all he could on the subject for the time being and had meant every word he said. Patience wasn't always one of his strong suits, but for Gemma he would be. Liam played to win because if he didn't he would lose it all.

He refused to allow for that possibility.

Liam clenched his hands open and closed several times. Gemma wouldn't leave him. He needed her. In time, she'd come around. He wouldn't think about the possibility of losing her. It just would not—could not happen. Instead, he'd concentrate on the upcoming ball. At least he'd be able to hold her in his arms as they danced. He'd achieved that goal, and he'd attain them all. Liam looked forward to each battle because in the end they'd both win. They'd have each other always.

After several moments, the carriage came to a halt in front of the Silverton residence. The carriage door opened, and Liam stepped out. He reached in and offered his hand to assist Gemma. With a delicateness ingrained in her she placed her hand in his. He helped her out, and they walked inside to attend the ball.

So far, Liam believed the night progressed towards meeting every one of his expectations. Soon he would be able to hold Gemma in as they danced in the waltz. A tingle of energy flowed through his veins, an awareness of her beside him. His fingers itched to reach out and just touch her, draw her close to him.

In the past, he dreaded the possibility, but now he looked forward to it with a glee he couldn't explain. Happiness bubbled inside him and hope filled him to the brim. Nothing could ruin this night for him.

CHAPTER TWELVE

*G*emma walked alongside Liam as they strolled towards the opening of the ballroom. They waited until they were announced and made their entrance for the first time as husband and wife. Gemma found the moment incredibly ironic. At one time, she would have given anything for them to enter on each other's arms as a married couple.

Now all she wanted to do was cringe when the announcement was made.

Small gasps and whispers filled the room. Heads turned to stare at them as they walked into the ballroom. Gemma held back tears from falling. She knew her marriage to Liam would be a shock to the ton—but she'd hoped that it wouldn't cause too much of a stir. A futile endeavor it seemed as eyes followed them throughout the room. Gemma didn't doubt they were all gossiping about them. Instead of letting them see how much it bothered her she held her head high and pasted a smile on her face. Outward appearances would go a long way into making them think they had no power over her.

Pain stabbed her chest as she sucked in a breath of discontentment. No, she would not think of things she couldn't change. Liam may be her husband, but she refused to allow him access to her innermost feelings. He gave up that right and Gemma rejected any possibility of allowing him to know how much she still loved him. Even though a tiny part of herself realized she still hoped for him to love her in return. That forthcoming collision of dueling emotions threatened to surface, and she needed to escape him if she had any chance of getting it under control.

She looked over and spotted Pearla and found the excuse she desperately sought to leave Liam's side. Pearla looked over at her anxiously, and Gemma knew she must have questions. She probably already received her invitation to the schedule dinner party. The time had come for her to explain her newly married state to her second best friend.

Lily would always be her first and the one person she told everything to, but Pearla had filled up a hole in her life with Lily's absence.

"If you will excuse me I see a friend I've desperately wanted to talk to for some time," Gemma told Liam.

"I will escort you there."

Why couldn't he just let her go off on her own? She didn't need him to watch over her every move. Gemma needed some space, and Liam's hovering made her feel closed in.

"You don't need to. I can find my own way."

"I insist. I would like to meet your friend."

Gemma opened her mouth and closed it into a pursed, straight line. Her gaze skirted over the crown and the prying eyes. They all seemed to wait for something to erupt between her and Liam. Did they know her marriage was a farce? Gemma refused to give them the show they appeared to be expecting. She didn't want to provide the ton with anything else to gossip about. No doubt they had already wondered about her hasty marriage. That at least she could brush off with the marriage contract Liam had procured miraculously. Gemma nodded in agreement and twined her arm with Liam's. If he wanted to deliver to her friend's side, she'd allow it.

Once they reached their destination, she could send him on his way. She led her husband over to where Pearla stood and introduced them.

"Liam, I would like you to meet my dear friend, Miss Pearla Montgomery. She is. I hope, going to join us for dinner in a couple of days." She turned to her friend and smiled brightly. "Pearla, my husband, Liam Marsden."

"It's nice to meet a friend of my wife," Liam said. A charming smile grew on his face as he bowed to her. "Perhaps you will honor me with a dance later."

"Oh, well. I don't know." Pearla looked up at Gemma. After she had nodded in approval, Pearla looked back at Liam. "I suppose that would be all right. I can fill you in for the second dance. I assume you will want to dance with Gemma first. It is a waltz."

"I do indeed. If you will excuse me, ladies, I see a friend I haven't seen in a while. Gemma, I shall be back soon to dance with you. I would also like you to mark me down for every waltz."

Gemma's mouth hung open. She had closed it quickly before anyone took notice. Every waltz? Liam was most definitely losing his mind. It wouldn't do, and she'd have to make him realize what a mistake that would be. She looked down at her dance card and the dances scheduled for the evening. They had several dances planned—three of them waltzes.

"That's a bit much, Liam. People will talk if we dance that many times. I'm supposed to leave it open for other men to dance with me."

"I don't care. I claim them as my right. I'm your husband, and I refuse to share them all with other men."

Liam's lips were set in a firm line. The color of his eyes darkened to a deep blue. His jaw clenched, locking into place as his eyes became firmer—demanding he be obeyed. Was he jealous? No, he had no reason to be. He was just being his usually over-bearing self. Still, it was... nice. Maybe he wanted her, and this was his way of expressing it. Gemma tilted her head and studied him.

Perhaps he did, but the man needed to be disabused of the notion he could dictate to her. She opened her mouth to tell him just that and thought otherwise. It wouldn't do to put him in place with words. Actions spoke volumes, and she'd find a way to get through to him. It was best just to appear to acquiesce to his wishes for now.

He'd learn—the hard way.

"Fine. I will put your name down for them all."

"Good. I will take your leave now."

Gemma glared at his back as he retreated across the room. Dance every waltz with him? Not going to happen... Someone else was just going to have to dance one of them with her. A man brave enough to stand up to her husband as he could be a little intimidating. All she needed was time to locate a gentleman willing to dance with her. Liam would be angry, but she could deal with it. Gemma would allow her husband to have two of them. He'd just have to accept one had to go to another man. She hated when people gossiped about her.

"Your husband is quite the charming fellow, now please explain to me how you happened to find yourself married to him," Pearla said.

She looked at her friend and admired her golden blonde hair. She had it pulled back into a chignon; tiny tendrils of wispy curls framed her face floating around her ears and neck. Her cerulean blue eyes glowed with anticipation and concern. Her heart-shaped face tilted inquisitively as she waited for Gemma to answer her question.

"It's a long story." Gemma sighed.

"Well lucky for you I have plenty of time. I have lots of questions. It's nice to finally be able to talk to you. I have to admit I was rather surprised by the hand-delivered invitation. I didn't even know you were no longer at the country house of the new Earl of Devon. How did that little weasel react to your marriage? I would have loved to witness that."

Pearla hated Alfie almost, if not more, than Gemma did. They had taken an instant dislike for each other. It probably had something to do with his lecherous nature and her unyielding independence. Pearla was not encumbered with a guardian. The sum of her wealth was inherited from her grandmother without any stipulations. She was the only unmarried female free to do whatever she wished without answering to a male relation.

"Alfie thought to marry me himself."

"I heard he racked up quite a bit of debt and ran through all of the money he inherited with your father's estate."

"Indeed he did. He thought marrying me would help him get out of debt. It probably would have temporarily until he wasted all of my inheritance."

"So how did you get out of marrying him? I assume by latching on to that handsome devil you married, but how did that go about?"

How to answer that? Did she tell her friend the complete truth or continue to deny what her heart constantly tried to beat into her head?

"Liam is very handsome. Don't let that fool you. He can be just as devious as any man." Gemma sighed and considered her next words. "But he also has a protective streak to go along with it. If not for him I don't know where I'd be right now."

"Oh, I'm sure he can be. Most men are capable of it on some level." Pearla pinned her with her gaze. "You are dodging my question. What don't you want me to know?"

"A lot. I don't want to talk about it. Perhaps I should though. It would probably help to get it all out, and then maybe I can let it go. I'm not sure where to start."

"Try the beginning."

Gemma stopped and looked at the ground. She didn't want to discuss any of it. Unfortunately, she also knew she needed to let it out, or she'd burst. No one was better to converse about it with than her friend. She didn't have an invested interest in the outcome.

"That would take us back to before we met. When I was first introduced to Liam. He is Lily's twin brother."

"I thought they may be related. I was just not sure exactly how. Go on, explain the rest."

A dreamy look came over Gemma as she remembered the first meeting. Liam had been so incredibly handsome. His blond hair glowed in the sunlight, and his blue eyes burnt with unrepressed delight. He and Lily had been laughing over some joke she hadn't been privy too. That first glimpse ruined her for anyone else. She wanted to have him look at her with love and happiness.

"I fell in love with him the moment I met him and yet thought him completely unattainable. I squashed all of those feelings and thought I never had a chance with him. If you had asked me even a week ago, I'd still believe that. I still do if I am being honest. I don't know why he married me. The truth is he didn't have to, and I'm even more confused now that I ever was."

Pearla's eyes squinted with confusion. "I don't understand. He married you to save you from your cousin right?"

"Yes, he did."

"What other option did he have?"

"He could have escorted me to Lily," Gemma explained. "Of course, Alfie might have come after me there. I doubt he'd have let it go, but he wouldn't have been able to make me come back to England, once I was safely with Lily."

"Ah, I see your point. He could have made you

miserable though. Alfie's good at that. Maybe Liam has feelings for you."

Gemma shook her head. "No, I don't believe he does."

"Does he know how you feel about him?"

"Yes. Well, he did. I had this attack of conscience a couple years ago and thought of course I will never have a chance if he doesn't know how I feel about him. I confessed my love only for him. His eyes were cold as he looked down, said he didn't feel the same way and had no intention of ever marrying. Words can't express how crushed my heart was. I didn't think I would ever recover. Maybe I never did. I can't allow myself to trust what I feel, and I am even more leery of Liam."

"What a fool." Pearla placed her hand on Gemma's arm, attempting to reassure her. "Maybe he finally realized how much you mean to him."

It took everything she had not to laugh. It was so nice to have Pearla to talk to, someone so completely on her side. She needed this in the worst way.

"No. I think it is some misplaced duty to his sister. Lily asked her father to help me. She knew about Alfie's plans for me and wanted me to come live with her. Liam and the viscount devised a plan to help me escape and go live in America with her.

Something changed in Liam's mind when he arrived and saw Alfie attacking me." Gemma shook her head, cleared away the unwanted image of her cousin. "Liam didn't marry me because he has unrequited love for me. He did it to protect me from my horrid cousin. Running away wasn't the answer. Alfie would have chased me to the ends of the Earth."

"Do you still love him?"

Gemma started to fidget. Now was the time to admit how much she did need Liam. She didn't want to, but the time had come to be honest with herself. She had never stopped loving the dratted man. She couldn't breathe without thinking about him and the love still burning inside of her.

"Yes. I know I shouldn't. I am fighting every feeling I have for him. My mind keeps telling my heart to give up, but it still holds hope."

"I'm so sorry, Gemma. I can't be mad at him though. He did save you from that awful cousin of yours. I know you are miserable right now, but I agree with him." Pearla embraced her in a quick hug and stepped back. "Alfie would not have given up on attaining you for his wife if you had merely run away. He needed your money too much to let you go that easily. I wouldn't be surprised if he still had a plan hatching in his greedy mind."

"No doubt he does. I can't worry about that right now. I have more pressing concerns."

"Such as?"

"How am I going to get out of three dances with Liam? I am not going to give the ton any more reason to gossip about me. My hasty marriage is enough fodder for the gossip mills."

Just as she said the words, she spotted the Duke of Huntly arriving at the entrance to the ballroom. He was announced and made his way inside. How serendipitous... The duke wouldn't balk at standing up to her husband, and he'd no doubt readily agree to dance with her. She'd just fail to mention how Liam wanted to dance every waltz with her.

"Never mind I think I have an idea. I need to go speak to His Grace, the Duke of Huntly."

"You know him?" Pearla's mouth hung open with surprise.

"Yes. He is Liam's friend. He will be at dinner as well. You may as well meet him now."

"Really? Who else is going to be at this dinner party?"

"Only his parents. Have you met them?"

"No, I can't say I have. I look forward to it."

Pearla and Gemma walked over to the Duke of Huntly. He stopped before them and bowed. His black hair curled around his neck, and his eyes held a sadness that Gemma wished she could erase.

"Gemma, it's nice to see you here. Is Liam with you this evening?"

"He is. Were you looking for him?"

"I do need to speak with him. I stopped by, and Pemberly said he believed you were both here tonight. I don't like balls or any social occasions, if I'm being honest. I did receive your dinner invitation. I will, of course, attend."

Gemma smiled at him. He was a nice and charming gentleman. She looked over and found Pearla charmed with him and for the first time completely tongue-tied.

"Noah, please excuse my rudeness. This is my friend Miss Pearla Montgomery. Pearla this is His Grace, Noah St. John, Duke of Huntly."

"It's a pleasure to meet you, Miss Montgomery." Noah bowed.

"I'm glad you will be attending the dinner party. Pearla will be there along with Liam's parents."

"A nice intimate affair, good, I detest crowds."

"I hope I can talk you into at least one dance before you leave. I know you have pressing concerns with Liam, but I still have yet to fill up my dance card."

The duke didn't look happy at the idea of dancing. His face paled, and his lips formed a straight grim line. He looked all around the ballroom, everywhere except directly at Gemma. Pearla continued to nod her head at the appropriate times, but not once did she speak in the presence of the duke. Later Gemma would question her unusual silence, but now she had more pressing concerns.

"I suppose I can. Is it too much to ask for the first dance? I would like to leave as soon as possible. I don't want anyone to get any hopes up of my staying."

"You are in luck, Your Grace. I can write your name in for the first dance and it is about to start."

As the words left her mouth, the beginning strands of the waltz reverberated through the room. Noah hooked her hand in his arm to led her onto the dance floor. In the distance, she could see her husband enter the ballroom with a murderous look on his face. She knew she played with fire by dancing with Noah, but she was willing to get burned to get her point across. Liam thought she wanted his friend, and she didn't see any reason to disabuse him of that notion.

Just because she admitted to herself she still loved him didn't mean she shouldn't follow her instincts. Liam flat out told her he didn't have any feelings for her. Why should she believe he'd suddenly had a change of heart? Gemma needed to protect herself before she found herself unwilling to live without Liam. Loving him would only lead to her ruination. She refused to give into those unwanted emotions. All she wanted was a little distance—to be able to think clearly. Liam made her forget who she was, and she got lost in wanting him. If he believed she desired his friend perhaps she'd get some of that much needed space.

CHAPTER THIRTEEN

*A*s soon as Liam entered the ballroom after leaving his business acquaintance, he saw his best friend leading his wife to the dance floor. Never would he have guessed her intentions – had he known, he'd never have left her side. It was a total surprise to see Noah at the ball. When Noah lost his wife, his need to socialize also vanished. Without Rubina, he had lost hope and any wish to be around people. Especially around anyone that would fawn all over him because they believed he was once again the catch of the season. Liam had never envied his friend his title or properties. They came with adverse side effects.

He loved Noah like a brother, but at that moment all he wanted to do was murder him.

All right maybe that maneuver would be a tad extreme, but Liam had never before had rage coursing through his veins as it now did. He weighed his options and tried to decide what his next move should be. If he marched out onto the dance floor, he would create a scene that would forever be remembered. He didn't want to look like the jealous arse he actually was. He scanned the ball-room and saw Gemma's friend, Pearla on the outskirts watching them dance. With a plan of action in place, he strolled over to her side.

"I need your help."

Pearla jumped up, and her voice squeaked as she said, "What?"

"Dance with me."

"Um no, I don't think that is a good idea. I can tell you are rather angry. Don't be mad at Gemma, she was only trying to prevent a scandal. Dancing with her three times isn't a good idea."

Gemma must have told her that was her reason for wanting to dance with Noah. Pearla didn't realize that his wife had developed an attachment to his friend in a very short period of time. Well, if she believed that he was going to allow her to further along that connection she would soon find out exactly how wrong she was.

"Is that so? Well, it may be a little late to prevent that. I wanted to dance with my wife and I will. Now come dance with me."

"All right, but I want my objections to this to be noted. It is a bad idea."

"Duly noted and also rejected. I don't care if it is a bad idea or not, it's going to happen."

Liam grabbed her hand in his and led her onto the dance floor in the middle of the waltz. He guided her along the floor until they neared Gemma and Noah. He weaved her around the floorboards as fast as he could without knocking into anyone. Once he spotted his intended destination, he did the necessary steps to arrive there.

"Now this is what is going to happen, Pearla. You are going to switch places with Gemma. I need you to dance with Noah so I can dance with my wife. Do you understand?"

"Yes, it is a horrid plan. Please don't make me do this. I beg you," she pleaded.

"Please help me, Pearla. I need to dance with my wife."

She stared at him for several seconds. "Do you love her?"

A lump formed in his throat. God yes he did.

Why couldn't he get his wife alone long enough to tell her? He nodded. "Yes"

She smiled. "I still think this is a very bad idea."

"What could you possibly have against switching places with Gemma? Most ladies would kill for a chance to dance with a duke." Liam knew she would do it. She'd have said no outright if she didn't want to help. His lips tilted into a half smile and teased her a bit."Noah won't bite, I promise. He will be a perfect gentleman. We are almost near them, be prepared to switch."

"I'm not most ladies. I have no wish to dance with any duke; in fact, I really don't want to dance at all."

Liam ignored her protestations and led her to the other side of the dance floor. Once they were next to Gemma and Noah, he twirled Pearla around until she almost collided into them. Both of them looked up in surprise, and Noah nodded in Liam's direction. He understood what his friend was after. They both did some fancy maneuvering and switched partners. Liam finally had Gemma in his arms where she belonged.

Only it hadn't been where she wanted to be.

Liam wasn't entirely sure what her motivations were. When he'd come to find her for their first dance, he hadn't expected to see her being led onto the floor by Noah. It's rocked him to his very core. He'd clenched his fists as spurts of heat spread through him. Now having her in his arms again he could feel that heat turn into something deeper. A longing to drag her closer so he could feel her body rubbing against his own. He wanted to brand her in every way possible. Gemma couldn't possibly just not want to dance with him because it might cause a scandal—Liam had to dig deeper. Whatever was driving her further away had to be eradicated. Letting her go was not an option he would ever entertain.

"What's this about you not wanting to dance with me?"

"I don't know what you mean. Noah offered and I accepted. He said he could only dance the first dance because he didn't like social events and had some things to discuss with you. I didn't think you would mind."

"Don't lie to me, Gemma. Your friend said you thought dancing with me three times would cause the gossip mill to start talking about us." Liam stared into her eyes. He wanted her to understand his position and how he saw the situation. "I don't give a damn what they say. They mean nothing to me. You will not do this again."

"You're taking this all wrong. This isn't something you should be concerned with. All I did was dance with your friend. That is perfectly acceptable."

Normally it would have been, but he knew how much she had flirted with Noah earlier in the day. He did not believe for a minute she had altruistic intentions. He didn't answer her because he had no words for her. Did she really expect him to believe that nonsense? Liam knew better. He had plenty to be concerned about. His wife was doing her utmost to avoid him. She didn't want to be near him.

All he wanted was to pull her close and breathe in her rose-tinted scent, skim his fingers across her silky smooth skin and feel her tremble with desire. Tell her how much he loved her—adored every inch of her.

Gemma appeared as if she couldn't wait to run in the other direction. She wanted to distance herself from him. Liam would give her anything in the world, except that. At the very idea of never seeing her again, shards of agony stabbed him through the heart. He needed to get her off of the dance floor and take her somewhere private. Tingles of sensation pooled inside him as a plan formed in his head. They needed to talk where ears were not privy to their discussion. Liam also had an unruly craving to kiss her, and that was not something anyone needed to witness. He twirled her around the dance floor until they reached the edge. He pulled her hand in his and led her away from the ballroom. Luckily, he was very familiar with the Silverton House so he knew exactly where to take her to have their conversation.

"Where are you taking me?"

Liam ignored her question. She would see soon enough where they were headed. He pushed open a door and pulled her inside. The door closed behind them with a quiet click. He turned to Gemma and reached for her. Now they could talk in private. She bit her lower lip and shook her head. Fear spilled out of her eyes, and she started to back away from him. Damn her and her need for space. Distance was the last thing they needed between them. Stalking toward her Liam decided what she needed from him at that moment was to know she belonged to him. She'd never belong to anyone else—she was his wife, the woman he loved beyond reason. Liam needed to claim her in the only way he knew how.

"Liam, what are we doing here?"

He stepped forward, grabbed her hand and pulled her into his arms. Once she was securely within his embrace, he fixated his complete attention on her. Gemma licked her lips and let out a breath thick with anticipation.

"You belong to me."

He leaned down and captured her lips with his. Her mouth opened, and he pushed his tongue inside. He licked hers with his as they dueled for control. A fierce heat ignited within him as he tasted her sweetness. Nothing would ever compare to her sweetness and Liam lost himself in the kiss. A soft moan filled the room. He wasn't sure if it came from him or Gemma, but it only encouraged him to seek more of her. His hands roamed over her back as he pulled her tighter into his arms. She leaned her head back and gave him better access to her sleek neck. He began to rain kisses down her throat and stopped just above her lace-encased bosom. He rolled his tongue over the top of the pearly white mounds and this time the moan that echoed through the room was hers.

"Liam, we should stop."

"No, we have only begun. I need more."

He wanted her completely naked, so she knew once and for all who she belonged to. Liam wanted to claim his wife and consummate their marriage, but she was right. This was not the time or the place to do it. Once they arrived home, they could continue where they left off. In the comforts of his bed, he would love her properly. When they were there, he would tell her how much she meant to him and that he couldn't live without her. It would be perfect and the most amazing experience of his life.

"Liam, please. Not now—No, don't stop, I changed my mind. Kiss me again."

Who was he to deny her what he wanted himself? With a newfound softness, he caressed her lips with his. As gentle as he could he showed her that he loved her with a simple kiss. He poured every ounce of what was inside his heart into that action, hoping, praying, and trusting her to realize what it meant. One of her hands roamed across his neck, and the other one rested on his hip as she tried to get closer to him. He breathed in her scent and memorized every aspect of this moment with her. It promised to be something he wanted to remember for the rest of his life.

As he made love to Gemma with his lips, he could feel her hands move from their positions. She cupped both of his cheeks with her hands and pulled away. She looked into his eyes and stared deep into them for several moments. Liam believed she was seeking an answer to a question that she desperately needed. While he pondered what that question might be something struck him from behind and threw him off balance. He fell to the ground and hit it with a small thud. The room span. Gemma voice called to him, his name echoing in the distance. Her voice seemed so far away, but he could see her blurry image right in front of him. What happened? What had struck him from behind? Who would ruin such a perfect moment? Liam struggled to remain conscious because Gemma could be in danger. In a minute, he would get up, he could do it. Blackness overcame him, and he gave into it.

CHAPTER FOURTEEN

Gemma watched as Liam crumpled to the floor. One minute she experienced a bliss only Liam could give her and the next she saw blood trickling down his forehead with him falling to the floor. It was the most surreal moment of her life. It couldn't possibly be happening. Gemma took a deep calming breath. She leaned over and brushed one of Liam's blond locks away from his forehead. His breathing seemed to be even. That had to be a good sign. Her hand shook as she caressed him one more time. Tears threatened to fall from her eyes, but she pushed them back. She couldn't give into such a weak and useless emotion.

Liam needed her help. If she was going to be free to get it for him, she had to take care of some unwanted business first. She stood up and clenched her fists at her side. Hatred coursed through her veins as she faced her cousin... She studied him and assessed the situation. How was she to handle Alfie? He didn't seriously think he'd get away with harming Liam. He stood off to the side and watched Gemma with an evil gleam. He held the statue he'd used to hit her husband firmly in his hands. He was tapping his hand with it in an aimless motion. He let it fall to the ground near Liam as he moved toward her. What could he possibly gain by harming Liam? Even if he killed him, that would not guarantee he could gain access to her money.

"Alfie, what are you thinking? You could have killed him!" her voice frantic as she thought about her next move. She took a few slow steps away from Liam's crumpled body. The more distance she put between him and her cousin, the better his chances were.

"I'm thinking, dear, that he does need to die."

"It won't help you to kill him. You must know that. As his widow, I gain complete control over my funds."

"As well as a good number of his too, I assume."

Gemma hadn't thought about what assets she would gain through her marriage. All she thought about was her own and that Alfie wanted her money to pay off his ever-growing debts. Did he see a way to get more than what she had? Of course, he did. If he could somehow coerce her into marrying him up on Liam's death, he would get whatever she inherited from him as well. He was a bloody fool because no way would Liam's father allow that to happen. Gemma continued to back away from Liam and the fool followed her, watching her every move to make sure she couldn't escape. Once she figured enough distance was between them she stopped. Liam lay still on the floor behind them both.

"You're an idiot."

"I don't think so. I am going to win, and you will help me. First, Liam needs to die."

No, Gemma wouldn't allow it. A world without Liam in it? She held her breath as the image took root inside her head. She wouldn't survive. If he died, she'd be lost. Alfie would not take him away from her. She'd just started to think it might be possible for them to have a real marriage. Liam could love her. He at least desired her. When he held her in his arms and showered her with kisses, she'd given in. She was tired of fighting her love for him. Gemma would rather stop breathing altogether than allow her cousin to kill the love of her life.

"No, wait. Think about this, Alfie. He doesn't need to die. I will give you all my money. Just leave with me now and I will make sure you get everything. I will even leave Liam and stay with you if that is what you want."

"I don't bloody want you. I just want your funds. I will take them and his. Rest assured I will enjoy you a bit before I kill you too. I plan on leaving England and never set foot in this rotten hell again."

"England isn't at fault for your foolish mistakes. Only you are. You can't run from yourself."

Alfie had clearly lost his mind. She had joked Liam had lost his when he insisted on marrying her. There wasn't any doubt in her mind her cousin truly was insane. How had she not seen it before? He would do everything he said to get what he wanted. He believed she owed him. If it saved Liam to go with him, she would, but she hoped it wouldn't come to that.

"I don't care what you think. I know what needs to be done. Now quit your babbling and don't move. I am going to kill your husband and then the two of us are going to leave this place as quietly as possible. We leave for France tonight."

Gemma saw a movement in the distance. Liam had started to wake up. She had to find a way to distract Alfie to allow him time to regain all of his faculties. What should she do? He told her to be quiet, but she suspected if she kept talking it would work as a good distraction.

"I don't see why I should go along with you. If you want to kill Liam I don't have a problem with that. You would be doing me a favor actually. I just hadn't thought that through." Gemma shrugged her shoulders, trying to give off the impression she didn't care. A bundle of energy burst through her giving her the strength of will to move forward with her plan. She prayed if Liam heard her words he didn't believe them. All she wanted to do was distract her evil cousin. "My intention had been to get an annulment, but by all means you should make me a widow instead. I won't be going to France with you though."

"You think what you want, Gemma dear, but soon you will realize that fighting the inevitable will prove futile."

Gemma circled around to the other side of the room as they talked. What could she do now? Talking wasn't working as a good enough distraction. A plan—she needed one. Gemma took slow concise steps until she stood near the fireplace and looked down at the nearby toolset. A quick action was needed. Alfie needed to be incapacitated. He'd never leave her and Liam alone if she just let him leave the room. A reasonable discussion was out as a means of getting through to him. Her cousin was insane and beyond reason.

Gemma moved to stand in front of the fireplace toolset and placed her arms behind her back. She reached down and, as slow as she could, grabbed one of the irons. Once she had a firm grasp on it she pulled it up as quietly as possible so that Alfie would be unaware that she had a weapon to use against him. The heavy statue he had used to knock Liam out still lay on the floor where he had dropped it. Gemma hoped he had no other weapon available. She started to move toward him with her hands behind her back while Liam still struggled in the background to get to his feet. He had made a little bit of progress as she gained access to one of the fireplace irons.

"I disagree. I would never willingly go with you anywhere. I would always fight until I had no breath left within me. You sicken me, and it disgusts me that you think I would ever allow you to put your filthy hands on me. You are insane and should be in Bedlam."

"I sicken you?" Alfie laughed. "Well, it's a good

thing I don't give a damn how you feel. Women are only good for one thing, and once I have it from you it won't matter anyway."

Alfie reached into his pocket, pulled out a pistol and raised it in Gemma's general direction. She stopped with barely two feet between them. She still had the iron firmly in her hands, but the pistol changed her plan.

"Are you going to shoot me now?" Gemma giggled manically. She couldn't seem to help herself. The panic welling inside her made her react in an odd way. "When you haven't gotten everything you wanted out of me yet? Like I said before you're an idiot."

"Oh, I'm not going to shoot you—yet. If I wanted you dead you would be already. I couldn't very well shoot Liam when he had his hands all over you. I might have accidentally missed and killed you instead." His smile made goosebumps spread all over her. The malicious gleam in his eyes sent shivers down her spine. "No, I had to knock him out first and kill him once I separated the two of you. Enough talking, it is time to say your final goodbye to your husband."

Alfie turned to see Liam had already risen to his feet. He was still a bit unsteady as he stared into

Gemma's eyes. She took advantage of Alfie's back being turned to her and pulled the iron in front of her and raised it up high. Just as she reached it up to swing at him, Alfie raised his pistol toward Liam, ready to shoot.

"Well look who decided to join the party. Are you ready to die, Liam? I owe you for that beating you gave me the other day. Did you really think I'd let that go?"

"I had hoped you wouldn't be so foolish as to try to kill me. Apparently my hope was a bit misplaced."

"Don't worry, you won't live long enough to stress over your own follies."

Just as Alfie pulled the trigger, Gemma swung the iron around hard and hit him in the shoulder. It jerked the pistol to the side forcing the bullet to graze past Liam and lodge in the wall. Liam leaned forward and knocked Alfie to the ground. He wrestled the gun away from him and bashed Alfie unconscious. Gemma raced into his arms and shook visibly. Tears flowed down her cheeks as she sobbed uncontrollably.

"You were so brave. It's okay. Let it all out. I'm here for you." Liam assured her, "If not for your quick thinking he would have hurt us both."

"I couldn't let him hurt you. We need to get out of

here. I can't be in the same room as him. Take me home Liam."

"I want to take you home. I need to have you safe there, but first we need to make sure he'll not hurt anyone else ever again. You understand that right?"

"I do. But I can't be in this room." Gemma's arm shook, and she rubbed her hands up and down trying to dispel the tingles. "I will leave and go get someone to help. Stay here and make sure he doesn't wake up and try to escape."

"Yes. That's a good idea. Go see if Noah is still here. He will know what to do."

Gemma nodded and raced out of the room. She entered the ballroom and found Noah talking to another gentleman she didn't know. She hurried over to his side and tapped him anxiously on the shoulder.

"Oh Gemma, there you are. I wondered where you and Liam disappeared to."

"I need your help. Liam, he is in a room." Gemma spoke rapidly and in short bursts. "The library I think. My cousin attacked us."

"Say no more. Show me where to go."

"No, you need to get the constable. Alfie is subdued for now, but if we let him go this could happen again."

"I will send someone to get them and then we will go back and help Liam. Is that okay with you?" Noah asked.

"Yes, but please hurry."

Noah walked off in the opposite direction and spoke to one of the servants. Gemma watched as the servant nodded and then took off to follow his directions. Noah returned to her side after the servant left to do his bidding.

"All right, Gemma, take me to where your husband is waiting."

"Follow me."

She led him to the room and when they entered, she saw her cousin was still unconscious. Liam held the pistol in his hand and kept a close eye on the fallen man, a grim look on his face.

"Gemma tells me you two were in a spot of trouble and here I thought you were off to a more pleasurable evening."

"It started out that way" Liam smiled. "But then it went to hell pretty fast."

"I sent a servant to get the constable. They should be here shortly to arrest the man. Why did he attack the two of you?"

"He wanted to kill Liam so he could get his hands on my money," Gemma said.

"Greedy bastard," Noah said in a scathing tone.

"Broke. He is bleeding debt and needed it to get solvent again. Before I married Gemma, he planned on marrying her to get his hands on her money. I thwarted his plans, and he decided I needed to die because of it."

"I see. Well, it looks like money is going to be the least of his worries soon."

They sat in that room for almost an hour before the constable arrived. He asked a bunch of questions and determined that Alfie needed to be arrested. After a time, he would go on trial and most likely be sentenced to prison or sent to a penal colony to serve out his sentence. It didn't matter to Gemma as long as she never had to lay eyes on him again. This was one experience she never wanted to live again.

"Can we go home now, Liam?"

"Yes. I think it is time we went home where I know I can keep you safe. At least we know he won't be bothering us ever again."

"That is a small comfort right now. I haven't exactly stopped shaking from the whole experience."

"In time it will get easier. Don't expect it to happen overnight though. I need to go talk to Noah for a quick minute and then we will leave."

Gemma watched as Liam walked over and talked

to his friend. Noah nodded and turned back to talk to the constable.

"What did you ask him?"

"If he could take over here so I can take my wife home."

"I take it he said yes."

She certainly hoped she'd read the situation correctly. Gemma didn't ever want to lay eyes on her cousin again. All she wanted was to curl up in Liam's arms and wrap up in his warmth. He made her feel so protected, almost loved. For now it was enough, it had to be. She wouldn't give Liam up without a fight.

"He did indeed. He also said I owed him and to expect to pay up at that dinner party you planned."

Gemma smiled, in all of the chaos she had forgotten about her dinner party. She also made a decision when she saw Liam lying on the floor bleeding from the head wound Alfie had inflicted him. She would tell him she loved him and never stopped. It was time for her heart and mind to quit fighting.

CHAPTER FIFTEEN

*L*iam helped Gemma into their carriage. The entire way out of the Silverton Ball Gemma didn't utter a word. Her face was devoid of all color but her green eyes held the luminosity of a dull jewel. Liam didn't know what to do to shake her out of this state of numbness.

When he had regained consciousness and saw Alfie brandishing a pistol in her general direction his heart had stopped beating for a second. It had taken him longer than he would have liked to regain his equilibrium. If not for her quick thinking, he might not have made it out of the situation alive. The bullet had grazed him, leaving a streak of blood on his arm as it passed by and embedded itself into the wall behind him. Gemma had saved his life by striking her cousin with the fireplace iron.

"Everything will be all right. We just need to get you home." Liam tried to reassure her.

Gemma leaned her head against the side of the carriage and closed her eyes. Liam hoped she wasn't closing herself off to him. He needed her now more than ever. This fight for control they battled over, since they married a couple days ago, must end tonight. Gemma didn't trust that he could love her. He saw that now. She believed that he only married her to protect her from her cousin's nefarious intentions. Now that Alfie would never be a problem again she could very well find a reason to bolt. Lily would always welcome her in South Carolina. Liam had to stop her before a plan formulated in her mind. Gemma couldn't leave him—he wouldn't allow it.

If she left, his heart would not recover from the loss. He was such a bloody fool. How could he have not realized sooner how much he loved her? Why had he been so damned stubborn? Gemma was his everything. Without her, his reason for being would be obliterated. He had to fix this mess once and for all. The path that must be taken was clear to him. It had always been obvious what must be done. He had only put off the inevitable. Tonight, once he had her safely in their home, he would make sure he'd tell her he loved her. When she was ready to accept him, he would show her exactly how much.

Once he spilled out all of the emotions welling up inside him, and if then she still wanted to leave him, he'd have to find a way to let her go—wait hell no, he wouldn't let her leave him. Liam couldn't believe he'd even considered giving in and stepping aside. He'd just keep pushing until she admitted she never stopped loving him. Liam refused to believe her love for him didn't still fill her heart. When you truly love a person, it doesn't go away.

The carriage came to a complete stop. Liam looked out the windows and saw the outline of his townhouse directly in front of him. They had finally arrived home. The footman opened the door, and Liam stepped out. He reached his arms back in and picked Gemma up into his arms. She slumped her head on his shoulder and wrapped her arms around his neck. Her skirts dragged on the grown as he carried her up the steps and inside their home. He nodded at Pemberly as he walked inside.

Gemma was way too complacent. Why didn't she argue more? She wasn't acting like her normal self. He had to get her to snap out of whatever world she'd retreated too. He needed his fiery Gemma with him.

"I don't want to be disturbed the rest of the night."

"I will see to it sir," Pemberly replied.

Still carrying his wife in his arms he walked up the stairs to his bedroom. He refused to be separated from her another night. From this night forward they would never be parted again. He pushed open his door and strolled over to his bed. He set her down on top of the bed and with extreme gentleness caressed her cheek.

"Please say something. I need to make sure you are okay," Liam pleaded with her.

Gemma looked into his eyes, and he noticed that at last the glassiness had started to abate and a little life had started to show in their depths. She raised her hands to cup his cheek inside her palm. Green eyes surveyed him while her other hand reached up and skimmed over his superficial wound.

"You could have died," she whispered. Her hands shook as she studied the blood staining his shirt. "Because of me. My cousin was going to murder you to get to me..."

"But I didn't. This is not your fault." Liam touched her cheeks with the palm of his hand, making her focus her eyes on his. "I'm here. I'm safe. Because of you. You're the bravest person I know. You fought him every step of the way."

"No, you're wrong because of me you were a target." Gemma shook her head. "Alfie never would have shot you otherwise. I had to do something to help. I kept him talking as long as I could. I said some things…"

"I know they were not true. You would never wish me dead," Liam reassured her.

"Do you? Really? I haven't exactly been nice to you the past couple of days. My heart hurt so much, and I reacted instead of stopping to think about what my words and actions might do to you. I'm so sorry."

"You have nothing to apologize for. Stop saying you are sorry. I'm not."

Tears fell from her eyes and trailed down her cheeks. Liam wiped them away with his fingertips. "Yes, I wish I could have avoided hurting you, but I wasn't ready for your love. I wish I had been, and we could have avoided this whole mess. If anyone should be sorry, it's me, but I can't be. Do you want to know why?"

"No. Yes. I don't know." Uncertainty shown through her eyes.

Liam laughed. "I will tell you anyway. I'm not sorry because as crazy as this path has been it led me to the exact place I was always meant to be. Right here with you. We will be stronger because of everything we have gone through. This means the rest should be easy or as easy as we make it. No matter what life throws in our path we can get through it as long as we stay together."

"How can you be so certain?"

Liam lifted her hand and placed a small kiss in her palm. He gazed into her eyes, attempting to pour all the emotion he felt into her. She needed to believe in his sincerity.

"Because I love you."

What he didn't say to her was that he believed she could still love him too. In that moment, it didn't matter if she didn't say it back. He needed to let her know how much she meant to him. Her well-being and what she needed to get through this moment was his top priority. The time for them to stop and share how they each loved each other, and how much, could be saved for another day.

Liam cupped her face in both of his hands and placed a light kiss on her lips and stepped back from her. He held his hand out to her, and she looked up at him apprehensively. She appeared to be gauging his reactions and trying to determine if it was all real. Her head tilted to the side, and her lips opened as a small breath released from her lungs. She looked down to his hand and then back up to his face directly into his eyes. A small smile formed on her face as she placed her hand in his. He pulled her off the bed and into his embrace. He leaned down and captured her lips with his once again. Her arms slid up his chest and wrapped around his neck. The kiss deepened as they touched their tongues together, mimicking a dance. The beat of his heart thump faster inside his chest as he continued the kiss. Gemma's hands roamed to his hair as she ran her fingers through them; pulling him closer as they each fought for control.

Liam pulled back and turned her around. With agile grace, he started to unpin her hair and pull it out of the braid so expertly weaved. Once every strand was loose he fanned out her sanguine curls over her back and shoulders. The silky strands were heaven on his fingertips. Pushing the strands aside, he placed small kisses along her shoulder to the base of her neck. With each kiss, he unlatched one of the hooks holding her dress together until it draped open revealing her corset. Liam pushed the dress down, and it pooled at her feet. He yanked at the laces of her corset until it loosened enough for him to remove it. He spun her back around to face him. She stood before him only wearing her chemise. Her face no longer pale, but flushed bright and rosy; her green eyes sparkled with desire and her pink tongue darted out and slid over her plump lips. She reached for him, and he wrapped his arms around her once more, needing to feel her in his arms.

Their lips met in mutual desire. Kissing and touching each other was the only thing that mattered to Liam at that moment. He had waited so long to have her in his arms. It had only been a short amount of time, but to him it had dragged on for an eternity. He lifted her up and her legs circled his waist. He walked them back over to the bed and sat her down on top of it. Gemma untied his cravat and yanked it off his neck, throwing it over his shoulder. With a wicked gleam in her eyes, she pulled his shirt up and ran her fingers across his chest. Liam groaned at the feel of her hands on his bare chest. He pushed her backward so that she lay on the bed and pulled his top over his head. The rest of his clothing followed soon afterward and he returned his attention back to his stunning wife. While he had been divesting himself of his clothing, she had removed hers as well. She lay on his bed in all her wondrous glory. For a brief moment, time stood still as his gaze took in the sight of his beautiful wife.

"You're so alluring," he whispered. "I want to taste every inch of you."

Gemma laughed as he crawled in bed next to her. Her nipples tightened into tiny nubs inviting him to bring them into his mouth. He ran his tongue across one as he pinched the other one between his finger and thumb. A moan of pleasure could be heard throughout the room. Gemma liked having him touch her beautiful bosom. Liam switched over and brought the other tight nipple inside is mouth and licked. He pinched it with his teeth and soothed it again with a gentle sucking of his mouth and lips. Trailing his other hand down across her stomach it rested at the apex of her legs. He caressed the curls he found there with the palm of his hand and stroked the sensitive nub with his thumb. Gemma's breathing became more ragged, and the sounds of pleasure coming from her encouraged him to explore even more. He slid down the bed and pushed her legs apart. With as much tenderness as he could he licked her core and suck the nub into his mouth. Gemma squirmed and tightened her legs around his shoulders. Liam kept licking and stroking her with his mouth, tongue, and fingers. It didn't take long for her to scream when she found her source of ecstasy.

"That's amazing. We must do that again."

Liam laughed and crawled up to lay next to her on the bed. Her face glowed with a languidness that showed the aftereffects of her orgasm.

"We're not done yet."

"I know, but I liked that. I'm not so sure I will like the next part."

"I'll be gentle. It's only the first time that hurts. After that, it will be nothing but pleasure I promise."

"I trust you, Liam."

Liam kissed her as he stroked her breasts with his hands. He positioned his body over hers and pushed one of her legs up to accommodate his large size. She wrapped the other leg around his hips. One slow inch at a time, he pushed himself inside her. He could feel her begin to stretch and welcome his length. After a few excruciating minutes, he reached the barrier marking her a virgin. He looked down into her trusting eyes and gave her a moment to adjust to what was about to happen. She reached up and twined her hands around his neck and pulled him down for a sweet kiss. Liam decided to distract her with his lips while he pushed all the way inside of her. Gemma stiffened as he broke through, and he placed soft kisses across her face and neck. She needed a little bit of time to adjust to his size. Once she started to move underneath him, he took it as a sign to begin thrusting inside of her. Slow at first, he moved almost all the way out of her and then just as slowly, he went back inside. He had done that for several strokes before she thrashed with wild abandon. Liam lost control and moved at a much faster pace until he felt her channel start to tighten on him with tiny ripples and Gemma screamed as another orgasm wracked through her body. He followed soon after with an equally intense release.

Liam rolled them onto their sides and withdrew himself from her body. He didn't want to leave her because everything had an incredibly right feeling while he was buried deep inside her.

He had finally made love to his wife, and it had surpassed all of his wildest imagination. He couldn't' wait to do it all over again. He pulled a bed sheet over both of them as he snuggled closer to her. Gemma's head rested on his shoulder a contented smile on her face. Liam didn't want to be anywhere else than in that room with her nestled beside him in bed. With that though drifting through his mind, he let himself fall into a deep sleep.

CHAPTER SIXTEEN

Gemma woke up, warm and comfortable, enclosed within Liam's arms. Lifting her head, she looked outside and saw the sky was still dark. Moonlight beamed through the window and bounced across Liam as she turned to gaze at his sleeping face. She couldn't have been asleep very long before something startled her awake. Her throat closed up tight with an unidentifiable emotion. Shallow, rapid breaths emerged from her mouth. She raised her hand to her chest as sharp pinpricks stabbed her. The panic that shot through her took root at her center and spread throughout her whole body. She needed air and to think. Staying in bed with Liam would not allow her that freedom.

No decisions could be made with him sleeping beside her. It didn't make sense, but something had snapped inside her. Gemma needed to get out of this room and gain some distance from Liam...

He almost died because of her. She looked down at her husband's sleeping form. He deserved better than her tumultuous feelings. How could she love him so much it hurt and still need to find some distance from him to think?

Because of what her cousin almost did to him, he was probably better off without her in his life. What if Alfie escaped justice? He'd just keep coming after them. Gemma needed to make sure Liam would never come to harm again because of her. She didn't want to leave him, not really. She just needed to be sure of him and his professed love. If she could establish that once and for all, she'd be able to accept her place at his side.

They needed to have a conversation that didn't involve him kissing her senseless.

Gemma slowly extricated herself from Liam's embrace. A bedsheet tangled between her legs and Liam's arm held her tight against him. First she needed to find a way to unravel the sheet from her legs. Once that small task was accomplished, she could move out of her husband's arms. She twisted her legs until the sheet loosened and then as carefully as possible slid out of bed. Gemma knew that Liam's injury had been minor, but she still didn't want to interrupt any healing sleep.

Perhaps it was a tad ridiculous when the wound hadn't even needed any bandage. The bleeding had stopped before the constable arrived, and it appeared to be no more than a scratch under direct scrutiny. She couldn't help from worrying about possible long-term damage. Any injury could lead to larger and more pressing issues. She didn't want anything to happen to Liam just because she couldn't sleep and developed an enormous case of anxiety.

After crawling out of the bed, Gemma took a minute to assess the situation. Her dress lay in a green pool of satin and lace on the floor next to the bed. Her chemise lay shining like a bright white beacon a few inches next to it. She could put that on and sneak over to her room to grab her wrapper. Everyone in the household probably still slept, but the servants would probably be getting up soon to start their daily chores. She didn't want to give them something to gossip about. Gemma knew she was being unrealistic, but she didn't like anyone talking about her. Her marriage to Liam hadn't started out the best and she couldn't deal with their wagging tongues. In time spending the night in her husband's bed would become commonplace, for now, though it was something she wanted to hold close to her heart. It wasn't the servant's business when her husband made lover to her.

Grabbing her chemise she put it on as quickly as possible, and tiptoed out of the room. She closed the door with a soft click and continued to her room. Once she arrived at her door, she pushed it open and hurried inside. The drapes were spread wide open at the windows in the room allowing the moonlight to highlight areas of the bed. Her wrapper lay on her bed next to her pearly-white silk nightgown. She grabbed both of the items and put them over her chemise. At least on the outside it would appear like she hadn't been sleeping naked for the past couple of hours.

Making love with Liam had surpassed anything she could have anticipated. If she were honest with herself, she hadn't known what to expect, but she knew she loved him and wanted to express that with him. When he had told her he loved her, for a brief moment her heart stopped and her ears rang. Her whole body went numb and then she could feel the echo of her heartbeat against her eardrums.

Liam loves me...

She repeated that over and over inside her head and still didn't quite believe it. The whole thing just didn't feel real. The dreamlike quality forced her to pinch her arm. She squeezed the skin between her fingers, and the small stab of pain ensured her that everything happened.

"Ouch." She let out a small quiet squeak.

Gemma exited her bedroom took quiet steps down the stairs. She needed to find something to occupy herself with. Anything...as long as it wouldn't let her dwell too much on the things that kept her awake; she should be upstairs still asleep in Liam's arms. Gemma couldn't help but think that not everything was as settled as she would like them to be. Something still nagged at her, and she didn't know how to explain what it was.

At the bottom of the stairs she realized she had a tiny problem. She had no clue what to do with herself. She could go to the library, but the light outside and inside wasn't exactly conducive to reading. The past couple of days had been filled with chaos and stress, and it started to affect her ability to reason properly. No matter, she could still relax on the settee in the sitting room and think about what she wanted or rather what she expected from her marriage. She already made her decision. It was not a matter of how to proceed with it. She would worry about the particulars later; right now, she could go to the library and have a glass of sherry to alleviate her anxiety. As she turned to stroll to the library, she bumped right into someone and knocked them down.

"Oh, I'm so sorry. I didn't know you were there." Gemma apologized.

Janie sat on the floor looking up at her. Her skirt fanned out around her as her legs peeped out from underneath it. Gemma reached down and offered her hand to help her to her feet. Once Janie was standing, she smoothed her skirt and addressed what was on her mind.

"No, the fault is mine, ma'am. I should have made my presence known. I saw you walking down the stairs and thought you might need something," Janie said.

Gemma thought about it and maybe it was a good thing she bumped into Janie. She could help her with a few things. Food being one of them as she suddenly .

"I'm a bit hungry and thirsty. I thought everyone

would be asleep still." Gemma bit her lip after the words spilled out of her mouth.

"Everyone has been asleep for hours. I woke up about a half hour past to start my day. Pemberly usually awakes around the same time. He should be rousing soon. What can I get for you?"

"I'd love something light to eat. And some milk? Whatever you can find available is fine."

"Would you like me to bring it up to your room? Or perhaps *another* room?"

Janie no doubt referred to Liam's room. She was too good of a servant to be so indifferent about the situation. What she wanted to know was if the new lovers, her and Liam, wanted a meal to share after their strenuous lovemaking. She was wrong, of course, not about them finally consummating their marriage, but that she wanted something to share with Liam. No, he needed to rest, and she would not disturb him for anything. Maybe she should have thought about his possible health before they fell into bed together, but sadly all she could think about at that moment was how much she needed him. While deep in those incredible moments, her feelings brimmed over the top and she rejoiced being alive. The rest was all second thoughts and worries for a later date.

"My room is fine. When do the servants awaken for the day?"

"Everyone should be up and moving in about a quarter hour."

"Oh really, that soon?"

"Yes. We do get up early to run the house."

"No, that's not what I mean. I just didn't realize how late or early it is depending on how you look at it..."

"Ah, I think I see what you mean. I will have a maid bring you up a tray to your room."

Janie turned to leave to do as Gemma wished. Her back was fully to her when Gemma had an idea.

"No, Janie wait. Can you just send my maid up without the tray? Have something sent to the library in an hour. A light meal like we discussed and plan on joining me. I have a few ideas I want to deal with for the dinner party tomorrow evening. I will need your thoughts on it."

"Very well, ma'am. I shall see you in an hour in the library." Janie turned on her heels and left.

Gemma strolled up the stairs to her room. She wanted to make the dinner party something even more special than she had already planned. It could be the wedding dinner they hadn't had. It was perfect because the most important people in their lives were already going to be there. The only person that wouldn't be in attendance was Liam's sister, her other best friend, Lily.

She wished Lily could be there with them. Gemma missed her a lot. It couldn't be helped though, and she wouldn't dwell on something that could not be changed. Liam promised her a, and she intended on holding him to that promise. With a little help perhaps she could make the arrangements herself.

The door opened, and her maid peeked her head into the room. She looked a little surprised to see Gemma awake at such an early hour.

Her eyes were wide, and her mouth opened up as if to let out a small "oh".

She didn't remark on whatever thought crossed her mind. The maid fully entered the room and stated her reason for being there.

"Ma'am Janie said you needed me."

"Yes, I need you to help me dress for the day. My hair is a mess, and I will need my maid to help me brush it out so it can be plaited. I have a lot to do today, and I need to get started on it right away."

"All right. Where would you like to start first? Dressing or your hair?"

"Let's work on my hair first. It will take the

longest to get through, and I told Janie to meet me in the library in an hour."

Her maid nodded, and Gemma walked over to sit down at her vanity table. Gemma grabbed one of her combs, and the maid grabbed the brush. They both started the long process of untangling her hair. Once all the knots were out, the maid quickly plaited her hair and twirled it into a bun at the nape or her neck. Her hair done Gemma walked over to her armoire and pulled out a dress. She stepped out of her nightgown and threw it on her still made bed along with her wrapper.

"Oh, I left my corset in Liam's room. I am going to go without one today."

Gemma was a bit embarrassed to admit she left clothing in her husband's room but decided to let that go. The servants knew anyway and she had nothing to be uncomfortable about. After her gown was laced up, she dismissed her maid. The maid wasn't needed at the moment for the rest of her plans. Gemma followed her out of the room and headed to the library for her meeting with Janie. As she descended the stairs, she could see the sun starting to rise through one of the hall windows. She smiled to herself knowing that she had a surprise in store for her husband. That is if she managed to pull it off in time for the dinner party. No matter what, she intended to make sure everything would go just right. She needed to tell Liam she still loved him, and this was the first step in making him know that it had never changed. Her heart belonged to him and it always would.

CHAPTER SEVENTEEN

*L*iam woke up and reached across his bed to locate his wife. As he spread his fingers over the soft sheet, he realized his hands hadn't located what they were in search of. He opened his eyelids to mere slits and looked over to the other side of the bed. Yes, it was empty, and Gemma had once again vacated the bed before he had awakened for the day. Two days in a row, she had managed to sneak out of bed without waking him to her intentions. The first night he made love to her, after the ball, it had been wonderful. She needed to stop this insane habit of waking up at the break of dawn. He wanted her wrapped in his arms so he could love her again in the early morning hours. When he saw her later that day, he would let her know how much this practice of hers disturbed him. Her penchant for early morning hours was not the only thing that bothered him. It had not escaped his notice that she hadn't told him she loved him. Again that is... What she said in the past was irrelevant to the here and now. He didn't know if she *still* loved him. It made him a desperate man and he needed to hear her say the words once again.

He might as well get up and start his day. Rolling over, he disentangled the sheets from around his body and crawled out of bed. He went to his armoire and grabbed the first pair of trousers he could find. After he pulled them on, Liam retrieved a shirt and pulled it over his head. Once he was fully dressed, he walked out of his room and went down the stairs to his study. He had a lot of work to do and a short amount of time to get it done. He had sat there for most of the morning before the overload took its toll on him. A sharp pain beat against his skull, as if a carpenter fast at work hammered away inside his head, making thinking a difficult endeavor. Liam rubbed his temples to dispel the thrumming deep inside his head. The last time this kind of pain visited him was when he'd had the idiotic idea to drink away his problems. He hadn't done that, so he didn't understand why the throbbing insisted on finding a home behind his eyes. Perhaps the stress of his life finally caught up with him and took up permanent residence.

"Looks like something is troubling you."

Liam looked up to see the Duke of Huntly, Noah walk into his study. His dark hair disheveled and his blue eyes twinkling with devilment. A lopsided grin on his face, the duke strolled over and sat down in a chair in front of Liam's desk.

"I have a lot on my mind. What can I do for you?"

"Are you sure you have time to help me. It looks like you have enough here to keep you busy for the next year or so."

"I can make time. If not for your help the other night I would have been stuck at the Silverton Ball far longer than I would have liked. I do owe you a debt of gratitude for wrapping up the Alfie mess."

Liam really did owe Noah quite a bit for dealing with that. If he had had to stay any longer that night, he might have just murdered the new Earl of Devon. It still bothered him the man had the gall to try and kill him to get his hands on Gemma. He broke the quill he held in his hands while thinking about breaking Alfie's neck instead. It snapped in two before he knew what happened.

"A little frustrated still by it all, I see."

"That's quite the understatement."

"How are things with Gemma?"

"Good. I think. Better at least."

"Well, that is an improvement over the other day when you were drinking your troubles away. Have you finally told her that you love her?"

Liam watched as Noah sat back in his chair and crossed his arms over his chest. His blue eyes pierced him with the question. That subject was the very one that troubled him the most.

"I did." His response barely a decibel above a whisper.

Noah raised his eyebrow in query over his response. "It didn't go well?"

"No, it went just fine. The only problem is—she never once said she loved me."

"I thought you believed she does. Did something happen to change your mind about that?"

"No. Yes. I don't know. I have doubts. She may still care about me, but I'm worried that she doesn't love me anymore. I may very well have destroyed my chances two years ago."

"Because when she professed her love you ran

away like a scared little school boy?" A rumble of laughter echoed through the room as Noah held his chest while it rumbled.

"Don't make fun of me. You would have too."

"On the contrary, I married the love of my life as soon as I found her." Sadness laced Noah's voice.

"I know. I can't imagine your pain when you lost her. I think my heart stopped beating when I saw Gemma in danger that night. I don't know what I would do if she died. Thank the Lord that didn't happen. I'm sorry I made light of your feelings. I know more than anyone how much you loved Rubina. I hoped you could find someone else, not to replace her, but to at least fill a bit of the hole in your heart."

"I don't think that is possible. She filled it to the brim, and when I lost her she left an empty shell. No one could ever truly fill that gap. I will probably marry again someday, but never again for love. I would like children though so when I think I can stomach it I will attempt to find someone at least bearable to live with."

Liam understood what his friend was feeling more than he wanted to. It just wasn't fair that Rubina died and left him alone. Not entirely alone, but some things just didn't measure up to the person you loved most in the world.

"I hope soon. I'd like our children to grow up as friends."

"I can't make any promises."

"I don't expect you, too. Just expressing my own selfish desires." Liam smiled.

"You are not selfish. I hope things work out with you and Gemma. That is part of the reason I am here."

"I don't understand."

"I just had an extensive meeting with the constable regarding Alfie."

"Really? I didn't know that it all hadn't been settled already. What did you discuss with him? Do I need to go and talk with him as well?"

"We had a lengthy discourse on the merits of stripping him of his title and shipping him off to a penal colony for the rest of his miserable life. The constable agreed. Alfie is no longer known as the Earl of Devon. That honor will befall to your first-born son."

"My own son is going to outrank me?" Liam asked. "That's as ironic as it is incredible."

"He considered just bestowing the title on you but

believed this was a better option. Once you inherit your father's title—hopefully sometime in the very distant future—you can change the succession rules to have it go to your second son. The paperwork is all being drawn up. There is some obscure rule in the line of succession with the Earl's title that allows it. The entailment on your title ends when you inherit it. That allows for you to make the necessary changes."

"What if I only have one son? This seems all a bit crazy."

"Then you don't need to make any changes. You can just let him inherit both. I'm just explaining all of your options. With the Earl of Devon's title, all of the properties entailed come under your control as Gemma's husband. It's not pretty though, as Alfie beggared the estates in a short time. You are going to have to work some miracles to make them profitable again."

"That's astounding. I don't have words for that. Gemma will be relieved her ancestral home is going to remain in her family. I can't wait to tell her the good news."

"You also can move into the country house if you wish to do so. As the guardian of the estate, it's your right to oversee personally all of its operations. That very well could take some personal and immediate attention."

"We may do that after the season is over. It's a busy time of the year for Marsden Shipping. I still need to finalize the merger with RandCo. Speaking of personal attention, I think I'm going to have to travel to South Carolina to meet with him to iron out some of the final details."

"Have you discussed that with Gemma?"

"No, I am not positive I need to go yet. I owe her a wedding trip, perhaps this can double as one. I know she wants to visit Lily so she shouldn't be adverse to the idea. I'm hoping that if she doesn't love me now by the end of the trip she will."

"If you want my opinion, you are overthinking it a bit. Just sit down and ask her. What are you afraid of?"

What was he afraid of? He feared she'd come out and say point blank that she didn't love him anymore. Lust was an equally powerful emotion. Maybe that was all she had left to offer him. Liam's worst fear was losing Gemma before he ever had her. He scrubbed his face with his hands—what a bloody fool he was. How could he ever believe she still loved him? Perhaps she cared. Could that be enough for their marriage to work? Liam didn't know if he wanted to find out the answers to these questions. He might not like what Gemma had to say.

No, talking to her wasn't an option yet. He would give her time to acclimate to her new life and allow her the necessary space to love him freely. When she was ready to tell him of her own love, she would. He just had to pray she would open up to him—express her innermost feelings. Liam trusted her with the truth of his love. He had to trust her to come to him with her own. It would be one of the most difficult things he'd ever done. Gemma deserved the patience to come to terms with her emotions. She'd been brave enough once, and he was the one that ruined it in the beginning. He would give her the time she needed.

"She just needs time. I owe her that much."

"I can see your point. I hope you get the outcome you are looking for. In the meantime, I have a few things I need to do before tonight. I will see you at dinner later this evening."

Liam frowned, how had he let that slip his mind? He had a lot to get done before his parents and their friends descended upon them for dinner.

"All right. Thanks again for the information. I will contact the solicitors to see what needs to be done with the Earl of Devon's estate. I'll see you later tonight." Liam nodded.

Noah left the room, while Liam went back to his stacks of paperwork. He had to make a dent in it before the evening progressed. The amount of work would only double once he got his hands on the necessary information regarding his new responsibilities. Gemma would be happy to have her family estate back under their control. The extra effort needed to make it solvent would be worth all of his time to make her happy.

"Excuse me sir, but you have a missive from your father," Pemberly said as he entered the room.

"Bring it here. I might as well see what he wants."

Pemberly handed him the letter and left the room.

Once alone, Liam opened the note and let out a sigh of irritation. His father demanded his attention immediately. After pondering his instructions for several minutes, he stood up and adjusted his jacket as he strolled out of the room.

"Pemberly I need my horse brought around. I feel like riding and father needs to see me right away."

"It's already been brought around sir. I thought it might be important."

"Very good. Pemberly, I don't know what I would do without you."

"I'm glad to be of service, sir."

Liam walked out his front door. As soon as he descended the steps someone knocked him down from behind and shoved him into an awaiting carriage. All Liam could think before the world went black was: *who the hell is trying to kill me now?*

CHAPTER EIGHTEEN

*G*emma found it funny how the things least planned for could spring up at the most inopportune time, much like a marriage of convenience, or inconvenience depending on the point of view in question. For Gemma, marrying Liam had been an inconvenience at the time. Her mindset had since changed, but that didn't negate her original feelings.

Switching, rewinding, and rethinking her position did not come easy to her.

Yes, right now, she could be the happiest wife in England and wouldn't change her circumstances for anything. There was only one problem. She still had yet to tell Liam that she never stopped loving him.

The time just—well, just didn't feel right. So she had kept her lips sealed tight and left him in the dark. Perhaps it could be perceived as cruel, and Gemma generally didn't have a mean bone in her body. In this instance, maliciousness held no place in her heart. Even though Liam had told her he loved her, she still had doubts.

She wanted everything to work between them, which was why she continued to plan the surprise for the dinner party. In fact, she had a small meeting scheduled with Liam's father in a few minutes to iron out some of the details. Gemma decided that they needed time away to just be with each other. No hassles or stress-inducing activities allowed. It would just be the two of them for six whole weeks.

Gemma currently stood in the middle of the sitting room at Marsden House. She couldn't sit still and had taken her anxiety out on the rug. A path would probably be worn in the carpet from her frequent pacing back and forth in front of the window. It had been a while since she'd been in this particular room—a smile formed on her face at the memory. Ah yes, when Lily plotted to run away from home. She missed her best friend and could benefit from her advice. Gemma had a feeling she was making things much more difficult than then needed to be.

She shouldn't have anything to worry about...

When Gemma had helped Lily, she had not counted on the wrath of her friend's father, Viscount Torrington. She'd never had a reason to meet him much. All she'd know about the man was what Lily had told her. Now he was her father-in-law, and she was seeking him out for his assistance. Gemma did learn one thing from helping her best friend run away. Because of that instance, she both feared the viscount and respected him for the care he demonstrated for his daughter. That didn't stop her from standing up for herself. She didn't let anyone bully her anymore.

"I'm sorry to keep you waiting, Gemma. Would you like to come to my study so we can discuss this in detail?"

Gemma looked over to see Viscount Torrington standing in the doorway of the sitting room. He leaned against the door frame with his hands folded across his chest. His steely blue eyes watched her as he awaited her response.

"Certainly."

The viscount turned on his heels and sauntered out of the room. Gemma picked up the pace and hurried to follow him to his study. Once inside, he took a seat behind his big burgundy desk and leaned back in his chair. She sat down in a chair in front of his desk, her back straight and her posture perfect with her hands folded in her lap. No matter how nervous she was, she refused to let it show in his presence. The viscount reminded her of a predator waiting for its prey to show its weakness. Once that disadvantage was revealed, he would strike the killing blow or, in this instance, get her to cave to his will.

"So I began the arrangements you asked me to do. I have my ship prepared for you to set sail to South Carolina. I cleared Liam's calendar for the next six weeks. You will be free to go on an extended wedding trip and visit Lily. I do have a few things I want you to take her and my new grandson. I've included a letter which explains everything to her. I will make sure it is loaded on the ship for you to take with you."

"Oh, that is wonderful. Thank you so much for your help. I couldn't have pulled any of this off without your help."

"I did it for Liam. The boy is besotted with you, and I think this time will be good for you both. Not that I don't like you, but I wouldn't have done this if

I didn't know he would want it to happen. Plus I was going to ship the stuff to Lily anyway and this is easier. I can rest assured you and Liam will make sure it arrives to her safely."

Gemma tilted her head and studied Viscount Torrington. He acted all tough on the outside and no doubt he was whenever the situation required it, but she suspected he was soft on the inside—at least with anything concerning his family. The rest of them, he would stomp out of existence if necessary. No matter, the man was still a force to be reckoned with.

"I'm glad my plans work well with your own then. It is a mutually beneficial arrangement. When is the ship scheduled to set sail?"

"You will leave in three days. It will give you time to finish packing and have your trunks loaded on the ship. Liam is capable of captaining the ship, so I am going to leave that in his hands. He has sailed enough to learn that area of the business and since he enjoys it, it seemed like a good idea. He doesn't get the chance to sail with the ships anymore."

"Good. Is there anything else we need to discuss?"

"No, that pretty much sums everything up. I sent a letter ahead to Lily, so she knows to expect you.

They should be there to meet you when your ship sets anchor in Charleston Harbor."

Gemma nodded. Everything was beginning to fall into place. The only thing that needed to be done was to tell Liam how much she loved him and that they are going to go on that wedding trip he promised her. Probably a bit sooner than he had planned, but that is what made it a surprise, she hoped that he liked it.

"All right, then I will take your leave. I have a few things to do at home before tonight's dinner party."

A half smile formed on his lips as he stared into her eyes. She didn't know what that smile meant, but she didn't think it was necessarily a good one.

"Before you leave Pia wanted to talk to you."

"Oh. I suppose I can wait and talk to her. How long do you think..."

"Okay, I'm here. Sorry it took so long. Did you tell her yet?"

Gemma looked as Lady Torrington came breezing in the room like a strong wind rolling over everything in its path.

"Tell me what?" Gemma asked.

"I've told her about the particulars concerning the ship, Lily's package, and how long they can expect to be gone."

"Oh good, I can tell her the good news then." Lady Torrington smiled.

"Good news?" Gemma asked raising her eyebrows. What were they up to?

"Yes. I'm coming along with you."

That wasn't exactly good news. Gemma adored Lady Torrington, but having her husband's mother along could be a bit of a damper on the wedding trip.

"With us?" The shock was evident in her voice.

"Oh don't worry, I'm not going to get in the way of your personal time, but I thought when Liam is busy captaining the ship we could spend some time together. It's been a long time since you visited here, and I want to get to know you again."

That didn't seem too bad, but still—

"I suppose we can do that."

What else could she say? Gemma couldn't be rude when they helped her out so much.

"I haven't seen Lily in three years. I want to see her and my new grandson." Lady Torrington placed a hand across her chest, a soft smile filler her face. "It's hard to believe my daughter is a mother now."

"You can also see that that package for Lily is safely in her care too," Viscount Torrington demanded.

"Of course. I didn't expect you to deliver it personally." Lady Torrington's gaze flew between Gemma and the viscount. "Oh, I see Thor implied that you would. He didn't want to spoil the news for me. I wanted to tell you myself."

Gemma gulped down a lump in her throat and nodded. It would be an interesting journey, one now she wished she could avoid. She couldn't believe they high jacked her wedding trip.

"Well, I look forward to the trip. I know Lily will be happy to see you. The only thing she would like more is if her father came too... You aren't coming too, are you?"

Viscount Torrington laughed when she looked over at him. He had been sitting quietly at his desk listening to their exchange. He had a very amused look on his face as he studied her. Gemma couldn't help but think they were planning something else. She didn't like the look on his face. He had a devious gleam in his eye that made them twinkle more than usual.

"No, I can't leave right now. Someone has to stay back and take care of the business with Liam taking off. I want at least one family member in England to see to any unforeseen issues. You can relax you won't have to entertain both of us for the journey to South Carolina."

"Oh good."

Torrington's laughter echoed through the room.

"Oh God, did I say that out loud?" Gemma asked.

"I'm afraid you did. Don't worry, we understand how you feel. Now you need to get going. We will see you tonight at your dinner party."

Gemma got up to leave. At the door, she stopped and glanced back at Liam's parents. They watched her, both wearing and identical mask of amusement as they waved goodbye to her. She started to question her idea to travel to see Lily. No, she wouldn't regret that. It would be good for her and Liam even if his mother tagged along for the trip. Plus there would be times when he'd be busy with captaining the ship and it would be nice to have someone to talk to. Gemma smiled as she exited the house and stepped into her awaiting carriage. Yes, everything was going well. Maybe not according to plan but definitely in the right direction.

Tonight's dinner party would be a new beginning for her and Liam. After she talked to him privately, they could entertain their guests and plan for their voyage. Nothing would prevent her from having it all. No one would ever come between her and Liam. She refused to allow anything to stand in the way of her and Liam's bliss. The rest of the trip home, Gemma went over everything she had to complete before the evening's activities. The first thing on her agenda was to locate her husband and finally tell him the truth. All her fears, doubts, and, above all, the love that filled her heart...

CHAPTER NINETEEN

*L*iam woke up in a dark room. Rolling over to his side he could feel the hard exterior next to him and pulled himself up to a sitting position. Leaning his head back against the wall behind him he blinked several time in an attempt to get his eyes to adjust to the darkness. After several minutes, he could make out shadows of objects placed within the room. A desk and chair were located on the far side of the room. Directly underneath him, the surface descended down into softness as he pressed into it. Roaming his hands in front of him he realized he laid on top of a bed.

The room appeared to sway from side to side in a gentle motion. From the little information, he had available he deduced he'd been placed on a ship.

What he didn't understand was why. He needed to explore his environment for more clues. The more he knew, the better his chances of extricating himself from these circumstances were. He moved around the bed and stopped when he realized the lump in front of him moved as he placed his hands on top of it. Skimming across the bed he could feel the moderate rise and fall of the person's chest as they breathed.

Who did they throw in here with him?

With as much care as he could muster he checked the person to make sure they were all right and to try to ascertain their identity. He skimmed the surface, and roamed over a person's body, it didn't take him long to realize he had been getting familiar with a woman's body. As a small moan filled the room, he backed away from her to gain some distance. He didn't feel comfortable touching another woman's body other than his wife's.

"Where am I?"

"Gemma?" Liam said, realizing exactly who'd been thrown in the room with him.

"Liam?" Bewilderment in her voice. "Where are we?"

"On a ship I think. I don't know why though."

Who could have put both him and Gemma on

board a ship—in a room together? More importantly why? None of this was making any sense to him.

"That can't be a good thing. Who would put us both on a ship?"

"I don't know" Liam shook his head. "I can tell you my first thought was Alfie had escaped, but I don't think that is the issue now. He wouldn't leave you with me."

"No, in his insanity he believes I belong to him. That still begs the question that someone kidnapped us and threw us here together."

"How did you end up here?" Liam asked.

"I don't know. I went to visit your parents and the last thing I remember was getting in the carriage to come home."

As that information processed in his mind, Liam started to wonder what or who might be the culprits of their predicament.

"That's odd. I had been on my way to visit my father when I got jumped from behind."

"Do you suppose they had anything to do with this?"

Liam pulled her into his arms and held her tight, breathing in her scent. At least, no matter what, they were in this together. He placed a light kiss on her forehead and pulled away from her. Having her in his arms was wonderful—but they had other pressing concerns.

"I don't know, but I think we need to get some light in this room and explore a bit."

Liam got out of the bed and began the slow process of discovering every aspect of the room. As he reached the desk, he ran his fingers across the surface until they landed on several items. One of those items was a box of matches, and the other was an oil lamp. With care, he opened the box of matches and struck one to light the lantern. He used the glow of the fire light to guide him in lighting it. Once the lantern was lit, he adjusted it, so a soft flush of light filled the room.

With the room illuminated by the light of the lantern, Liam searched the room for clues. His eyes landed on a parchment folded in half and resting in the middle of the desk. Grabbing it, he opened the note up and read it hoping an explanation would be enclosed. After he had finished examining it, he looked over at Gemma, puzzled about its contents.

"What is it?" She stood up and walked over to him.

"It's addressed to you. Here read it."

Liam handed her the note and watched as she read the words written on the page. He already played them back in his mind and wondered what it all meant.

Dearest Gemma,

By now you will have awoken and found yourself on board a ship. Please forgive us for our deception. I know this is not how you planned on making this voyage. It's not our intention to upset you or Liam. After a conversation I had with him a few days ago I realized you two needed help in solving your issues. You were taking a step in the right direction by arranging a surprise for him. Thor and I didn't believe it was enough and began to plan something on our own. Kidnapping you and forcing your hand seemed like a good idea. It worked for us after all. If Thor had never kidnapped me, I wouldn't have fallen madly in love with him. Our methods are a tad—underhanded, but our hearts are in the right place. We just want you both to be happy.

I know you will be devastated to realize I am not going to be joining you on this journey. We will just have to make up for that when you return home. I was sincere in wishing to get to know you better. Take care of my son, give Lily a hug for me, and give Baby Will a kiss. I trust you will still deliver our package to Lily when you arrive. It's why Thor explained how important it was to you in detail. Some things can't be explained in a letter, and some things are better done in writing. We hope in time you will look back on this with fondness and realize we did you a good turn.

You will be locked in the cabin until morning. The necessary items you will need are already in the room with you, including some food. The ship's captain will let you out (if you choose to leave the room) once the sun rises the next day. Use your time wisely.

Tell Liam how much you love him and let the rest take its natural course.

Love Always,

Pɪᴀ

P.S. Dᴏɴ'ᴛ ᴡᴏʀʀʏ about the dinner party you planned. We took steps to dismantle it already. Janie and Pemberly were extremely helpful in assisting us with our subterfuge. When you return, we can plan a new one.

"Yᴏᴜʀ ᴘᴀʀᴇɴᴛꜱ ᴀʀᴇ ʀᴇꜱᴘᴏɴꜱɪʙʟᴇ!"

"Yes, that is clear. What I don't understand is this surprise she speaks of."

Gemma nibbled on her bottom lip as she twisted her fingers together.

"I did plan something. It has some similarities to where we are, but no, this is not how I wanted things to go."

"So tell me what you actually planned."

She stopped in front of him and rubbed her hands up his chest. Winding her arms around his neck she leaned back staring into his eyes. Her fingers twirled through the ends of his hair.

"I wanted us to take the wedding trip you promised. I asked your father to arrange it. Of course, I didn't mean for us actually to leave for a few days."

"I like the idea of taking a trip with you" Liam smiled.

"Me too. Even though your parents went about this in a mad fashion, I'm glad they did."

"You are? Please elaborate."

"When I left Marsden House I was coming home to you. I have been putting something off because of my own fears and doubts. While I was there, I came to a decision to let it go and just be honest with myself and tell you what's on my mind."

"You doubt me? I know I gave you a reason to. I hoped that I put that to rest."

"It's hard to let go of feelings you have been carrying around for a long time. You dismissed my feelings as nonessential. It left me devastated, and it took me a while to crawl out of that despair. The idea of opening myself up to the possibility of revisiting those feelings did not appeal to me. It's the reason I have fought you every step of the way. My instincts screamed to put distance between us."

"I'm not running away now," Liam whispered. "I've been chasing you for days."

"I know. I'm done trying to escape the inevitable."

"Is that so?" Liam raised an eyebrow. "What do you want to do now?"

"It's time to open up and say the things I've been burying deep inside me. I've been the queen of denial for several days. No matter how scared and uncertain I've been, there is one blaring insurmountable truth."

Gemma placed her hands on both sides of Liam's face. She rose on her tiptoes and placed a soft kiss on his lips and took a step back.

"I love you. I never stopped. It's time to quit fighting something I can't control. Trusting you and believing you love me is the only option I have. You have always owned my heart."

Liam smiled when she finished saying the words

he'd been longing to hear. This is what his mother's letter alluded to. She knew that Gemma still loved him and was giving her a way to express it—albeit an extreme measure, but he found it endearing his parents' cared about the outcome of his marriage.

"I love you. I don't know how many times I need to say it for you to believe me, but I will keep saying it until it sinks in, and you do."

"I do believe you. Only someone that loves me would put up with the emotional upheavals I've put you through."

"I'm happier than words can express. Since we've discussed everything, how do you suggest we use the rest of our time locked inside this room?" Liam wiggled his eyebrows.

"I don't know," Gemma took a step back and tapped her chin. "They said we had everything we need here. Do you suppose they left us some cards? Lily taught me how to play whist a few years ago..."

She couldn't be serious? Whist? Liam could think of a million things he'd rather do than play cards. Honestly, there was only one thing he wanted to do at that moment. It involved them getting naked and loving each other all night long. He couldn't wait to strip her of her clothes and love her as he craved to. If she wanted to play cards, perhaps they could make it more interesting... a game of whist where the loser had to forfeit pieces of clothing to the winner. Now that was a game he'd willingly play. Somehow, he doubted Gemma had that in mind when she suggested whist. He stared at her with disbelieving eyes until she finally began to laugh so hard she had to hold her stomach by wrapping her arms tight around the middle.

"You should see the look on your face. I don't think I've ever seen you look more surprised. This even tops when I told you I loved you for the first time."

"I don't find it so funny. You know what I want to do."

"Yes, I do. Which is why I suggested cards. Which maybe we can do later because I want to do exactly what you have on your mind."

"Oh, you can read my mind now?"

"No. I just know we are for once exactly in the same spot wanting the same things, and I want to take advantage of it."

Liam agreed with her. He reached for her and pulled her back into his arms. Gemma tilted her face up towards his and he pressed his lips to hers. Once her mouth opened, he took advantage and tangled her tongue with his. Their passion ignited, and he pulled her as close as possible as their tongues dueled for control. Gemma's fingers trailed across his neck and up to his hair, and she seized strands of it in a tight grip. Liam pulled back and could see a slight blush begin to creep up her cheeks. Leaning down, he traced the red stains with butterfly kisses down to her neck stopping only when he could hear her moan of pleasure. He took a step back so he could look at her flushed with passion.

"I love you, but I absolutely adore looking at you in moments like this. I look forward to loving you for the rest of my life, and I plan on taking my time and savoring each moment."

"That has to be the sweetest thing you have ever said to me."

"I mean every word." Liam's gaze held Gemma's. "My family has a tradition. Well, it started with my parents."

"Kidnapping?"

Liam laughed and pulled her back into his arms, "No. Well yes, there is that, but it's a different tradition I'm speaking of. When we were children, my parents used to tell us a fairy tale. At the time, we didn't know they were telling us their story. I'd like to do something similar with our children."

"That's a lovely tradition. At what point would

we start our story? Once upon a time a gentleman saved a lady from a nefarious villain?"

"No, our story goes back even farther than that." Liam shook his head. "I'd start with once upon a time a gentleman foolishly ran away from the only lady he would ever love..."

Gemma's face softened into a delighted smile. Liam never wanted to cause her heartbreak again. From this moment on he would do his best to ensure her happiness. Leaning down, he kissed her again to finish what they started mere moments ago, loving his precious sanguine gem...

EXCERPT: A HIDDEN RUBY

A MARSDEN ROMANCE BOOK FOUR

DAWN BROWER

PROLOGUE

"*I* no longer wish to live... Without my love, I have nothing."

Rubina Leone St. John, the Duchess of Huntly meant those words. Without Noah... Her head fell forward hitting the palm of her hands. Tears streamed down her face. How could she go on without the only man she'd ever loved? If Paolo Fonte, Duca d'Sordillo, told the truth, her husband was dead.

"Don't be dramatic, Rubina." He held his hand over his heart. "On my honor, I will always take care of you."

She lifted her head and stared at him through hooded eyes. What a fool. Did he honestly believe she'd willingly stay with him? Her heart would always belong to Noah. No other man would fill the empty void his loss left behind. Slowly, she stood and faced him. With all the strength she had left, she spit in his face.

"You'll never take the place of my Noah." She returned to her seat. Rubina had better things to do with her time than deal with Paolo. He proclaimed to love her, but he'd kept her a prisoner for months in a tiny room. Only coming to visit her so he could stare at her while declaring his love. You don't imprison someone you supposedly love.

Paolo pulled out a handkerchief and wiped his face. "You'll regret that."

"No, I only wish I'd have done it sooner."

He stormed over to her side and lifted her chin, forcing her to look at him.

"*La mia bellezza...*" He stroked his fingers through her hair. "Such beautiful golden-blonde hair—so silky to touch."

Chills ran down her spine and her stomach rolled with queasiness as he touched her. Rubina was not his beauty... She never would be his in any way.

"I don't belong to you. I never have. When will you accept that?" She stared up at him in defiance.

"Never?" He raised an eyebrow. "It is such a very long time, my love. You will learn to love me."

Rubina choked back tears. If Noah was truly dead—it didn't matter. Paolo could do his worst. No matter how hard she tried, her feelings would remain the same. Her heart remained untouched by his false charms...

"*Ti odio.*" She let every ounce of hatred pour out of her. Rubina didn't want there to be any doubt how much she loathed Paolo.

"No, you don't." His sinister laugh filled the tiny room. "My dear, you don't really know what hate is —but you will."

"How did Noah die?"

Rubina needed details to understand how he could really be gone. Her husband was a strong virile man, so full of life. She couldn't truly believe he was —she gulped down a lump in her throat—dead.

"If you must know, someone helped him along to his untimely demise."

"No..." Rubina gasped. "Please—tell me you didn't murder him."

"I'll tell you no such thing. I'm not about to start lying to you my dear." He shoved his hands into his pockets and rocked back on his heels. "It's best you get acclimated to our long life together."

Rubina wanted to die. That would remain true as long as Noah was gone. She had something to take care of before she joined him again. Paolo Fonte's life must end. He would pay for his sins—for hurting Noah. She would live long enough to see it happen. Once she sent him to hell, she'd allow herself to breathe her last breath. She could once again be with her husband. They could spend eternity in each other's arms.

"*Sei un bastardo malvagio*," she exclaimed. Duca d'Sordillo was an evil bastard. "One day your cruelty will leave this world. On that day I will rejoice."

"Say what you want. Your words mean nothing, but you will come around." He grinned. "Until then, please enjoy the accommodations.

He turned to leave. The door shut with a loud thud. Paolo turned the key, locking her once again in her tiny hovel. Such love he showed her. Rubina stared at the door with disgust. It didn't matter. She had a reason to continue living. Once she found a way to end Paolo's life her mission would be complete. He must pay for the atrocity he caused.

RUBINA GREW WEAK. She barely sustained enough strength to lift up her head. Paolo limited her food to bread and water—barely enough to survive. He was trying to get her to cave—give in to his demands. The evil bastard wanted her to willingly join him in his bed. It would never happen. To betray Noah in such a manner... No, she'd rather die. If she didn't gain strength soon, she'd get her wish.

"Duchessa..."

Her body rocked back and forth, shaking from an unseen force, but she didn't want to open her eyes.

"Please wake up, Duchessa."

Rubina's eyelids fluttered open to gaze into the dark brown eyes of a man she'd never seen before.

"Who are you?" She stared at him, puzzled. Maybe he was a new guard Paolo sent to watch over her.

"I'm here to save you."

Rubina shook and tears streamed down her face. She didn't want to believe it was true. She didn't know how long she'd been a captive in Paolo's home. All she wanted to do was go home—see her father and brother again. They were all she had left in the world. If only Noah...

Rubina cried harder.

"Duchessa, we must hurry."

She tried to swallow a lump in her throat, but it

was too dry. She let her gaze meet his again and voiced her fear. "Are you real?"

He nodded. "I assure you, I am. Can you walk?"

"I'm so weak…"

"We will go slowly. I will carry you if I must."

He helped Rubina to her feet and led her to the open door. She was about to leave her prison. How long had she been locked away from the world?

"Why are you helping me?"

"I work for your brother, Conte Leone." They made their way down the long hallway. He stopped at the top of the stone stairway. "My name is Arturo."

"Damian sent you?"

Her family still believed she lived? Why had it taken them so long to find her? Paolo insisted the world believed her dead—as dead as her husband. No more Duke and Duchess of Huntly—no more beautiful love story.

"I'm afraid not." He lifted her up into his arms. "Everyone believes you are dead. I'm here on a different mission. It's a miracle I learned of your existence."

"Grazie." Rubina hugged him. Her whole body shook with the weight of her emotions. "I feared I'd die locked in that room."

"No need for thanks. I'd do it for anyone." His mouth formed a firm straight line. "What the Duca d'Sordillo was doing to you was wrong."

Rubina didn't want to think about Paolo. She just wanted to get as far away from him as possible. Maybe she'd return to England... She loved her home. Italy still held a special place in her heart, but it also filled her with terror. If she had never argued with Noah, Paolo wouldn't have been able to hold her captive. Her only intent had been to return to Naples and visit her father. As soon as she stepped onto the ship heading toward Italy, Paolo's men had seized her. They took her to his ship and locked her inside. Somehow, he arranged to have the ship she'd been on to sink into the ocean's blue depths—sealing the belief of her death.

"If you're not here to rescue me, then what are you doing in Duca di'Sordillo's home?"

"He is believed to have ties to the Mafioso."

Arturo set her down and scanned the room. He pulled her hand into his and led her outside. They stopped in front of a carriage, and he helped her inside. Once Rubina was safely seated, he flicked the reigns to get the horses moving.

"Somehow it doesn't surprise me. He's an evil

man—and evidently a mastermind in the criminal underworld."

Arturo nodded. "That's what we believed. We had no idea the extent of his criminal activities. Conte Leone sent me to investigate. If he'd known you were here, he would have come himself and ripped Duca d'Sordillo apart."

Rubina didn't doubt it for a minute. Damian was ruthless when he needed to be. He had a high power seat in the government. He hated the Mafioso and sought to eradicate them from Italy. It was turning out to be a daunting task. The Mafioso themselves were shrouded in secrecy.

"Where are we going?"

"Do you know where you are, Duchessa?"

"Please, call me Rubina," she offered. "I owe you my life. To answer your question—I have no idea where I am or how long I've been here."

Arturo frowned. "This is not good, Your Grace." He shook his head. "You are in Sicily near Palermo. It's been three years since the Conte and your father believed you drowned aboard that ship."

Rubina gasped. "No, so long…"

"Your family—they will be so relieved to find you still live. Thankfully, your brother awaits me in a nearby port. We can escape with him and travel to Naples."

Damian was near? The fates had finally decided to step in and help her. If only they'd done so sooner —she might have been able to save Noah. Pinpricks of pain shot through her heart as a vision of her beloved floated before her. She missed him so much.

Arturo urged the horses to go faster. The wind blew through Rubina's hair. Soon she'd be with her brother again, and she could plot Duca d'Sordillo's death. He would pay for his sins. First she'd need to regain her strength. She would not be able to defeat him being so weak.

"We'll be to your brother's ship soon, Your Grace."

"Thank you. I'm so tired... Maybe I should sleep a little bit." Her head fell forward, eyes drifting closed. They flew open as she gazed over at him. "I thought I told you to call me Rubina."

"Yes, Your Grace, but I cannot. Please, stay awake. We will be there soon."

Rubina fought her body's need for sleep. Once they got to the ship and reunited with her brother she could give in. Arturo assured her it was near. Deep breath in, exhale, if she kept reminding herself, it all would still be true. If this was a dream, Rubina never wanted to wake up. Only one thing would make it perfect: Noah—alive and well.

The carriage came to a halt near a small pier. The night sky was dark as pitch with tiny white stars dotting the black canvas.

"Duchessa, we are here." He nudged her forward. "Come, I'll help you board the ship."

"I don't think I can move, Arturo." Her eyes rolled backward, and her eyelids fluttered shut. "I don't have much strength left."

"I will carry you." Arturo lifted her into his brawny arms.

The warmth engulfing her spread throughout her whole body. She'd been cold for so long. He nestled her, letting her head rest on his broad shoulder. It was so nice to be taken care of.

"I don't know if I can ever thank you enough," she muttered.

"Quit thanking me, Your Grace."

Rubina never would. He saved her from a living hell.

"What do you have there, Arturo?"

Damian! His voice was music to Rubina's ears. Arturo hadn't lied. He'd brought her to her brother. Rubina wanted to cry again, but she held it inside.

"I found your sister, Conte."

"What?" Disbelief etched through Damian's voice. "You lie, my sister drowned aboard a ship several years ago."

"No, Conte." Arturo shook his head, jostling Rubina's head forward. "She lives. Duca d'Sordillo has kept her locked in a room for years."

Rubina lifted her head and met eyes that matched her own. In the moonlight, his silver-gray irises glowed in front of her. Damian gasped. *"Dio mio*, it's true..."

"Hello, brother."

Damian rushed forward and pulled Rubina out of Arturo's arms. His hug so tight breathing became difficult. "I can't believe you're here. If I'd known..."

"I know, please, I can't breathe."

Damian let her go, never once taking his gaze off of her. She understood because it all seemed like a dream to her too.

"Rue, oh God—Noah. How are we going to tell him?" Damian rubbed his hands over his face. "He is about to get the shock of his life. We must get to him fast."

"What?" Rubina gasped. "Noah lives? Paolo told me he murdered him."

"I assure you, your husband is alive and well." Damian nodded. He paced back and forth in front of her. His agitation making her nervous. "There's something you should know… He's set to remarry."

"No..."

Noah was hers. No other woman would lay claim to him. She had to get to London and reclaim her husband. How dare he move on when she suffered so much? She'd believed he was dead, and still she didn't give in to Paolo. When she got there, Noah would rue the day he'd ever thought to replace her.

Order Here

ABOUT THE AUTHOR

USA TODAY Bestselling author, DAWN BROWER writes both historical and contemporary romance. There are always stories inside her head; she just never thought she could make them come to life. That creativity has finally found an outlet.

Growing up she was the only girl out of six children. She raised two boys into productive young men. There is never a dull moment in her life. Reading books is her favorite hobby and she loves all genres.

She is active on Facebook, Twitter, and Instagram. To follow her or can find more about her check out her website for the pertinent information:

www.authordawnbrower.com

If It's Love (Amanda Mariel)

Odds of Love (Dawn Brower)

Believe In Love (Amanda Mariel)

Chance of Love (Dawn Brower)

Love and Holly (Amanda Mariel)

Love and Mistletoe (Dawn Brower

Bluestockings Defying Rogues

When An Earl Turns Wicked

A Lady Hoyden's Secret

One Wicked Kiss

Earl In Trouble

All the Ladies Love Coventry

One Less Scandalous Earl

Confessions of a Hellion

Coming Soon

The Vixen in Red

Marsden Descendants

Rebellious Angel

Tempting An American Princess

How to Kiss a Debutante

Loving an America Spy

Marsden Romances

A Flawed Jewel

A Crystal Angel

A Treasured Lily

A Sanguine Gem

A Hidden Ruby

A Discarded Pearl

Novak Springs

Cowgirl Fever

Dirty Proof

Unbridled Pursuit

Sensual Games

Christmas Temptation

Linked Across Time

Saved by My Blackguard

Searching for My Rogue

Seduction of My Rake

Surrendering to My Spy

Spellbound by My Charmer

Stolen by My Knave

Separated from My Love

EternallyMyDuke

Kismet Bay

Once Upon a Christmas

New Year Revelation

All Things Valentine

Luck At First Sight

Endless Summer Days

A Witch's Charm

All Out of Gratitude

Christmas Ever After

AFTERWORD

Thank you so much for taking the time to read my book.

Your opinion matters!

Please take a moment to review this book on your favorite review site and share your opinion with fellow readers.

www.authordawnbrower.com

ACKNOWLEDGMENTS

Thanks Victoria Miller. You're the best.

www.ingramcontent.com/pod-product-compliance
Lightning Source LLC
Chambersburg PA
CBHW050022180626
46810CB00002B/533